Cherished Wish

Cherished Wish

MELODY CARLSON

BETHANY HOUSE PUBLISHERS
MINNEAPOLIS, MINNESOTA 55438

Published by Bethany House Publishers
A Ministry of Bethany Fellowship, Inc.
11300 Hampshire Avenue South
Minneapolis, Minnesota 55438

Printed in the United States of America by
Bethany Press International, Minneapolis, Minnesota 55438

Library of Congress Cataloging-in-Publication Data

Carlson, Melody.
    Cherished wish / by Melody Carlson.
       p. cm. — (The Allison chronicles ; 2)
    Summary: Fourteen-year-old Allison finds herself the center of a custody battle between her glamorous, but neglectful, movie star mother and her long-absent artist father who wants her to live with him in a small Oregon town.
    ISBN 1–55661–958–8 (pbk.)
    [1. Divorce—Fiction. 2. Family life—Fiction. 3. Parent and child—Fiction. 4. Conduct of life—Fiction. 5. Christian life—Fiction.]
I. Title. II. Series: Carlson, Melody. Allison chronicles ; 2.
PZ7.C216637Ch   1997
[Fic]—dc21

                                         97–33853
                                         CIP
                                         AC

MELODY CARLSON'S many years of experience in working with children have formed the basis for her award-winning career as an author of nearly twenty books, most of them for children and young adults, including a SpringSong Book, *Benjamin's Box, Tupsu,* and *The Ark That Noah Built*. Melody resides with her husband and two teenage sons in Oregon.

Bethany House Publishers
Books by Melody Carlson

——————— ᙓᙓ ———————

THE ALLISON CHRONICLES

1. On Hope's Wings
2. Cherished Wish

ᙓᙓ   ᙓᙓ   ᙓᙓ

Awakening Heart
Jessica

To Carol, Robin, and
Renee, with love.

1948

One

AFTERNOON SUNLIGHT FLOODED the den with cheerful warmth. Allison glanced at the bookshelves that lined the walls, studying her grandpa's favorite room. It was such a painful reminder to her that he was gone. And as hard as it was for her to believe she would never see him again, it was just as shocking for them all to discover that James O'Brian, Allison's father, was very much alive and had been living out at the lighthouse. What a happy reunion they had shared when Allison and James returned to the house and surprised everyone there.

At the moment, James was scratching his head and rummaging through Grandpa's desk. At last he stopped and waved the familiar yellowed envelope. Allison knew it contained the letter she'd discovered in her mother's things in New York.

"This is it, Allison! My ticket to freedom! This letter proves those charges of embezzlement were completely false! I can't believe Marsha kept it hidden all these years—even during the war." He sighed deeply and shook his head.

Allison couldn't believe it, either. Why Marsha had allowed him to be blamed like that when she knew the truth all along was a mystery. Could she have possibly tucked it away and just forgotten?

James pulled some more papers from a heavy brown folder. "And here's the other letter you told me about, Allison. The one Father wrote before he—" James' voice choked and he sunk into the chair, gazing blankly at the documents spread across the desk. His head sagged slightly, and Allison knew the reality of

Grandpa's death was sinking in for him as well.

"I think I'd better take the kids home," Grace said. She had been sitting quietly in the corner, and she rose slowly, her eyes still fixed on James. "I'm sure they're exhausted from searching for Allison."

"I'm so sorry I worried you all like that, Grace," Allison said. Her secret trip to the lighthouse had given them quite a scare.

"It's all right, Allison. Under the circumstances, I can certainly understand why you took off without telling us. And it is wonderful to have James back—back among the living. It's just so unbelievably amazing—" Grace looked like she was about to cry again.

"I'm sorry, Grace. I invited you in so I could try to explain everything. . . ." James paused, running his hand over his father's desk. "But I'm having a hard time with all of this. I can't believe that I'll never see him again—" His voice caught slightly and he stared down at the letter in his hand. Allison could see that it was typed on Grandpa's stationery. The room grew hushed as he read silently. Allison tried not to stare at the tear that slid down her father's face. He wiped it with the back of his hand, then he set the letter down and looked up. "It helps to read this—it's almost as if he knew he was going to die. He actually took the time to write that he'd forgiven me, and he even asked me to forgive him."

"Dad, that's wonderful," Allison breathed. "Now at least we know he made peace in his heart before—"

"Hello in there," Andrew called, standing tall in the doorway. At sixteen, he was the oldest of Grace's three adopted children. Grace had told Allison how Andrew had taken charge of the frantic search for her, making the phone calls and such. "Muriel wants to know if everyone wants lunch." He winked at ʜ. "And we haven't eaten since last night, thanks to a certain renegade who shall remain nameless."

"Of course," James said as if coming to his senses. "You all must be starved! You will stay, won't you, Grace? No sense to run off just yet. You know how Muriel is about these things. Cooking is what she lives for, and she's probably slaughtered the fatted calf by now." James reached out for Grace's hand.

Grace's face flushed as she pulled her hand away. "Oh, I suppose . . . if it's no trouble. We don't want to intrude—"

"Grace, you know you're like family to us!" Allison exclaimed. "I'll go help Muriel."

Heather Amberwell was already sitting at the scrubbed pine table peeling carrots while her nine-year-old brother, Winston, bounced about the kitchen like an over-wound toy.

"It's about time, Allison," Heather scolded. "Did you think you'd get out of kitchen duty just because we all thought you drowned at sea?"

Allison laughed and marveled at Heather's ability to recognize people by their footsteps. "I was going to offer my help in here, Muriel, but Heather's being so sassy maybe I'll just—"

"You get right over here, Allison Mercury O'Brian!" Muriel commanded, wiping her hands on her apron. Muriel's face was still blotchy from their emotional reunion, and she grabbed Allison and embraced her for the third time that morning. Allison didn't mind one bit. "Now, don't you ever go running off like that again—you hear?" Muriel said in a voice that was supposed to sound stern.

Allison nodded. "I promise."

"Allison, it was really brave of you to take the rowboat out there in the middle of that horrible squall!" Heather exclaimed, tossing a handful of sliced carrots into a copper saucepan. One spun across the table, and Allison snatched it and popped it in her mouth.

"Ha!" Muriel remarked. "It was more a case of plumb craziness than bravery if you ask me."

"Allison?" Winston asked. "Is it true you rowed all the way out to the lighthouse in that awful storm? Weren't you scared? Didn't you think the mad lighthouse keeper would get you?"

"You bet I was scared, Winston, but Muriel's right—I was kind of crazy at the time. It's not something I'd ever do again."

Muriel sighed loudly, and Winston looked at Allison as if she were his new hero. She grinned and tousled his sandy hair.

"I'll set the table, Muriel," Allison offered. She carried the dishes to the dining room and opened the double-glass doors to let the sun in. Outside, the garden glowed with rich colors, and Allison breathed in the fresh sea air. It was good to be home.

An engine rumbled down the driveway, followed by the crunch of gravel beneath tires. Allison stepped out to see a large dark car followed by a black-and-white police car slowly pulling up to park. Allison hurried around the corner of the house just in time to spy her mother's secretary, Lola Stevens, climbing out of the first car. Allison cringed behind the thick laurel hedge as she watched Lola stride over to the police car and hand the officer a thick manila envelope.

If Lola thought she could take Allison back to New York, she had another thing to think about. Her father would put a stop to it. He had that letter now. He could prove his innocence. He'd know just what to do to send Lola packing. Allison dashed through the house and burst into the den, interrupting James and Grace, who were in deep conversation.

"She's here!" Allison gasped.

"Who's here?" James asked, noticing the fear in Allison's voice.

"Lola Stevens—Marsha's secretary from New York. She's here! She's going to take me away!"

"Calm down, Allison. We can handle this. I remember Lola. She wasn't an unreasonable woman." James headed for the front door, and Allison wondered if they were thinking of the same Lola Stevens. Grace slipped her arm around Allison's waist.

"Don't worry, dear. We won't let them take you—we'll fight them tooth and nail."

Allison gave her a weary smile and tried her hardest to believe Grace's words. James opened the door just as the bell rang.

"Lola," he said pleasantly. "It's been a long time, hasn't it?"

Lola's eyes popped open wide and her jaw actually dropped, revealing an unattractive double chin. "Oh my goodness! James O'Brian? Is that really you? I thought you were dead!"

"No, I'm quite alive, as you can see. Come in, come in. We were just getting ready to sit down for lunch. Care to join us?" James opened the door wider, revealing a uniformed policeman. James' friendliness caught Allison off guard, and Lola looked absolutely stunned.

"No—no, thank you," Lola stammered, struggling to gather her wits. "Where in the world have you been all these years, James?" she asked with undisguised suspicion.

"Well, Lola, it's a long story, and I'm certain the version you heard was not the truth."

Lola cleared her throat and straightened her short military-style jacket. Her hat was small and low on her brow, and if she only had a German accent, she'd surely have passed as a Nazi defector.

"I've come on a rather serious matter, James." Lola glanced over at Allison with steel blue eyes. "We've got a kidnapping charge against your father, a Mr. Riley O'Brian."

"I tried to explain to Miss Stevens here," the officer began in an apologetic tone, "that Mr. O'Brian just passed away last week and that he would never kidnap anyone."

"Regardless of that," Lola continued, "I have a legal document that clearly states Allison's custody is Marsha Madison's responsibility along with another letter declaring Marsha's wish for her daughter's swift return to Camp Wannatonka—as if she were ever there in the first place." Lola directed the last comment to Allison with a knowing look.

"Well, I have a couple of letters myself," James said. "And I plan to speak to a lawyer as soon as possible concerning my daughter's custody. In the meantime, Lola, don't you think it would be in Allison's best interest to stay here until this is settled? You know she's in good hands. Besides, Marsha is still on location in Istanbul."

"Where Miss Madison is has nothing to do with this, Mr. O'Brian. Allison must return with me now, or we will charge you with kidnapping—right, Officer?" The policeman looked at the papers and nodded his head reluctantly.

Allison stepped forward in anger. "What about me? Don't I get anything to say about this? I want to stay here with my dad! Can't you just tell Marsha that, Lola? If you make me leave him, I'll just run away again! I will, I really will!"

"Is this true?" James asked the officer. "Does Lola really have the legal right to take Allison even though I'm her father?"

"According to this court order. Frankly, I don't see a reason for it, but the law's the law. Unless Miss Madison gives some sort of special permission, the young lady will have to return with Miss Stevens here."

James clenched his fists and scowled. "I can't believe it! What kind of legal system takes a child from her father against her own free will just to dump her in a camp with a bunch of strangers?" The officer frowned but didn't waver. James' face was red and his eyes burned with anger. He turned and stormed off to the den, slamming the door behind him. Allison watched in dismay. Her father was supposed to help her—to save her from Marsha. What was happening?

"Officer," Grace implored in a consolatory tone. "Would there be any harm in waiting a couple days before Allison returns with Miss Stevens? After all, she needs time to pack, and she's been through quite an ordeal recently with her grandfather's death and all."

He nodded in sympathy. "Sure, I don't see a reason why she has to leave right this very minute. But don't let me down. Like I said, the law's the law. Come on, Miss Stevens, let's allow these people to eat their lunch in peace." He took her by the arm and, against her protests, practically pulled her down the steps.

"Thanks, Grace," Allison sighed. "But what am I going to do now?" The others gathered around, emerging from hallways and corners.

"We won't let that nasty old witch take Allison away!" Winston exclaimed, stomping his foot for emphasis. "Maybe we could make a booby trap for the next time she comes."

"Winston!" Grace reprimanded.

"But we have to do something, Grace," Andrew spoke up. "They can't take her because a stupid piece of paper says so—can they?"

Allison scowled. This was her home now, and she was tired of running. There must be some way out. But how?

The door to the den opened and James stepped out. "I'm sorry, Allison, but I had to leave. I was afraid I'd lose my temper if I stayed one moment longer, and that would only get us into more hot water. I have some good news, though. I just phoned my father's attorney in Port View, and he thinks we have a strong case. Unfortunately, he advised me to go along with Marsha for the time being. That's so Marsha can't use it against us later when we go to court."

"What do you mean, go along with Marsha?" Allison questioned, panic rising in her throat.

"I'm afraid we'll have to let Lola take you back for a little while. At least until we can sort this all out the right way."

"But how long will that take?" Allison moaned.

"I don't know. Maybe when Marsha realizes I have these letters she'll change her tune. But even if she doesn't, we can't give up. If we have to jump through rings of fire to get you—we will."

"Somehow we'll beat them at this," Muriel proclaimed from behind Allison. "In the meantime, lunch is getting cold. And if we're going to figure something out, we need some nourishment to help our brains work." In spite of herself, Allison smiled. Leave it to Muriel to suppose a good meal would drive their troubles away.

The room was quiet as they ate. Allison looked around the table. For once Grandmother Mercury's dining room looked as it should—full of people. And yet such somber faces. Andrew and Winston sat across from her, glumly poking their food. James and Grace sat at opposite ends, both deep in contemplation.

"Allison," Heather whispered beside her. "I read a story about a summer camp once, and I thought it sounded like such fun. Maybe you'll enjoy it after all . . . swimming and boating and . . ."

Allison sighed and shook her head. She knew Heather was just trying to cheer her up, but in this case, maybe Heather was lucky to be blind—she'd never have to go to one of those dreadful camps. "Oh, Heather, maybe I could survive that stupid old camp if I had you and your Pollyanna outlook along with me."

"That's it!" Andrew exclaimed. "Why don't we send Heather along with Allison! They'd have a terrific time together."

Heather laughed. "I'd love to go, but I'm sure they don't allow blind girls—"

"Why not?" Allison interrupted, catching Andrew's enthusiasm. "Besides, they wouldn't have to know you're blind—it's not like it's on their admission form or anything. And everyone knows you can do almost all the same things as the rest of us, and then some! If you came, Heather, it might even be fun!"

"Hold on now, girls," Grace said. "I'm not sure this is such a good idea."

"But, Grace," Allison pleaded. "You said yourself you always allow Heather to live a normal life."

"And if money's a problem," James chimed in, "I discovered a document regarding my father's will. It seems he's left everything to Allison and me. We could pay Heather's way."

Grace shook her head. "I don't know. I'm sure Allison would watch out for her. It's just that—"

"Oh, please, Grace. It'd be such fun!" Heather begged.

"Will you promise to be extra careful?" Grace asked doubtfully. James grinned across the table, then Grace chuckled and shook her head. "I guess I could let you go."

A cheer erupted around the table, and Allison squeezed Heather's hand. Suddenly, Camp Wannatonka didn't sound quite so horrible. But then Allison remembered her conversation with the young man she'd met on the train when she was traveling to Oregon.

"Dad, I met a boy on the train from New York to Oregon. His name is John Stewart, and he works at a Christian camp in northern Ohio. From what he described, it sounded really nice. I'm sure I still have the camp's address. Do you think there's any way we could talk Lola into this camp instead of cruddy old Camp Wannatonka?"

"I don't know why not—I'm sure it's worth a try. Maybe we should wire that camp in Ohio first to make certain they have space available, then we'll make the arrangements."

∞   ∞   ∞

The next day, Allison drove with her father up to the cemetery overlooking the ocean. She took a large bouquet of Grandmother Mercury's favorite roses and divided them between her grandparents' graves. She could hardly remember the foggy morning only days before when they'd gathered here for Grandpa's funeral. At that time, she'd had no idea that her father was alive. All she remembered from that day was a cold emptiness inside her. It seemed like another lifetime now. She stepped back and watched her father stand before the gravestones that marked the last link to his parents. The scene blurred in her own eyes, and she brushed a tear off her cheek.

"At least we still have each other, Dad," she said, slipping her hand into his.

"That's right, Allison. And I will not let them take you away from me. Never again."

When they returned home, Muriel met them at the door waving a telegram in her hands. "It's from the camp in Ohio!" she exclaimed. "They'll take the girls—they'll take them both! They want you to call at once to confirm their arrival time."

Allison hugged Muriel and dashed for the phone. "I've got to tell Heather!" she cried.

Later that evening, Allison and James ate dinner in the kitchen with George and Muriel.

"This clam chowder is just as delicious as ever, Muriel." James refilled his bowl with the thick, hearty soup.

"You were always such a good eater, Jamie," Muriel said as if James were still in knickers. "Here, have another biscuit."

"Muriel, I'll sure miss your cooking. Have you ever tasted camp food?" Allison spooned out a dollop of fresh strawberry jam.

George grinned. "Well, Muriel could fix you up some goodies to take—couldn't you, Muriel?"

"Of course! In fact, I've already started a provisions box for the girls."

After dinner, James sorted and organized a mound of papers from Grandpa's desk. Allison read for a while, but soon her eyes refused to focus and she got up to get ready for bed. She hesitated in the doorway for a minute, unsure of how to approach her father. "Dad?" she began. "Would it be okay for me to kiss you good-night?"

"It's more than okay, Allison. It's a requirement." She giggled and planted a kiss firmly on his stubbly cheek.

❧   ❧   ❧

The next morning, Allison and James were seated at the dining room table enjoying a leisurely breakfast. The telephone jangled noisily, and Muriel appeared in the dining room with a sour look on her face. "It's that woman again, Jamie. You'd better talk to her."

Allison could hear strains of the conversation, but her father's voice remained surprisingly calm and strong. He returned with a boyish grin, looking very much like a cat who'd just devoured a canary.

"So what's Lola think of our new plan?" Allison asked, eager to know yet fearing the answer.

"She thinks it's just fine." He sat down nonchalantly and sipped his coffee.

"Holy cow! Are you pulling my leg?" She looked at him in amazement. "What'd you do?"

"I just reminded Miss Stevens about some business she pulled behind Marsha's back ten years ago—some business I've kept to myself . . . until now."

"Dad, isn't that blackmail?"

"No, not exactly. I didn't make any threats. It was only a reminder. At the time, Lola told me she was doing it in the best interest of her employer, although I've had my doubts. However, I reminded her that we were also looking out for the best interest of her employer by trying to ensure the best interests of her employer's daughter."

Allison laughed. "Dad, you are brilliant!"

James frowned slightly. "I don't know about that, Allison. I can hardly bear to see you go. I know it's the right thing to do, but . . ."

"I know exactly how you feel." Allison swallowed hard. "I would give anything to be able to stay here with you."

"I remember my mother saying once that sometimes the only way to keep something is to let it go."

"She seems like she was a very wise woman," Allison said thoughtfully.

James smiled. "And you, my dear, are a lot like her."

Two

ALLISON STOOD BEFORE the old-fashioned oak vanity and checked herself in the mirror. It felt odd to dress up again, but she knew it was fitting for travel. She smoothed the peach rayon jacket and adjusted her straw hat, tucking a stray copper curl into place. She laughed as she remembered how she'd asked that New York hairdresser to dye her hair. It all seemed so far away now.

She looked around the bedroom—her room. She'd miss the sunny roses on the wallpaper and the pleasant window seat overlooking the garden, all cherished reminders of Grandmother Mercury. But she'd be back.

Downstairs, Grace and the Amberwells waited with Heather's bags stacked by the door. It was agreed they'd meet Lola at the Portland train station by noon. Allison felt thankful they didn't have to drive with her—it was bad enough they had to share the same train for several days. George and Muriel waved sadly from the driveway as James backed out the loaded Buick.

"Don't you two worry," Allison called out the car window. "I'll be back before you know it!"

"Allison, I'm so excited," Heather exclaimed before they'd reached the end of the road. "I hardly slept at all last night!"

"Me too. But if it wasn't for you, I'd be dreading this trip like the dickens. Heather, you look so nice—is that a new suit?"

"It was Grace's, but she did some alterations. Do you really like it? Let me guess—it's pink, right?" The girls giggled at the old joke, and Heather stroked the nubby linen fabric.

"You're wrong, Heather, it's mauve," Allison teased.

While James drove, they played twenty questions with Grace and sang along with Andrew and the radio. Allison had always dreamed of having a family like this, driving in a big car, laughing and joking and singing. It felt so good to be surrounded by people who loved her.

Allison looked out the window, hoping to imprint her memory with Oregon's exquisite scenery. She wanted to be able to instantly recall it in case she got homesick at camp, and she knew she would. She studied the rocky coastline with its clear blue Pacific reaching far into the horizon and majestic Douglas firs with lush ferns at their feet like fluffy green slippers.

"Allison?" James asked. "Tell us about that young man you met on the train—the one from this camp."

Allison instantly felt Andrew's gaze upon her. She blushed to remember her brief encounter with John Stewart. She'd been playing the part of a young woman on a journey when in actuality she was only fourteen and on the run. It hadn't taken John long to figure out she wasn't being completely honest with him.

"John was very nice," Allison began. "He's a lot older than I am . . . eighteen, I think. He has a sister my age, and he warned me to be wary of strangers while I traveled. He was right, but unfortunately I was careful of the wrong strangers." She told them about how her purse had been stolen in Omaha and how she'd suspected the man with the wooden leg. "Then when he caught the thief and returned my purse, I felt pretty foolish."

"Oh dear, I'm getting worried already," Grace said from the front seat. "I hardly know this Lola person. Will she really keep track of the girls, James?"

"Grace, don't worry," Allison assured. "Lola won't let us out of her sight for a minute. She's very dependable about her work. Marsha's her meal ticket, you know. Even if Lola doesn't like me, she won't let Marsha down."

James parked in the train depot lot. Andrew loaded the girls' suitcases and boxes onto a luggage cart. They entered the terminal, and suddenly Allison felt she couldn't bear to leave her father. As if sensing her fear, he took her hand and gave it a firm squeeze.

Lola strode up to them and glanced at her watch. "You're late, James," she said briskly. She tugged down her fitted blue jacket and checked the train tickets. Allison thought Lola's suit looked familiar, then she realized where she'd seen it before—in Marsha's closet.

"Here's Heather's ticket," Grace said to Allison.

"What do you mean, Heather's ticket?" Lola asked suspiciously.

"My friend Heather is coming to camp, too," Allison announced, no longer intimidated by Lola's domineering attitude.

"Well, I certainly don't intend to play nursemaid for two girls!" Lola exclaimed.

"We don't need you to play anything," Allison retorted. "Heather and I are perfectly capable of caring for ourselves—thank you very much!" She looked Lola square in the eye and Lola stepped back in surprise. Allison remembered her experiences with Lola back in New York. Lola had always treated Allison like an infant. Things would be different now.

"All aboard for the eastbound train," announced the station master. Allison hugged everyone good-bye, including Andrew. Then James held her in a long embrace.

"Allison, I won't let Marsha take you away," he whispered. "I promise—you'll be with me as soon as possible. Be brave." He held her tight, and it felt like her heart was being torn from her chest.

"I love you, Dad," she said quietly. She had told very few

people that in her lifetime, and only when she meant it.

"Hurry up, Allison," Lola commanded. "We don't want to miss our train."

Allison took Heather's arm and followed Lola up the steps to the train. They sat in first class by the window, and Allison waved sadly as the train pulled slowly out of the depot. She watched until her father was just a tiny spot in the distance.

Lola sat across from them in silence, flipping through a movie magazine. Her legs were crossed, and Allison watched one black alligator pump twitch from side to side like an animal waiting to attack its prey. Finally Lola looked up from her magazine and studied Heather as if sizing her up. Allison wondered if Lola had figured out that Heather was blind. She looked nervously from Lola to her friend. Heather looked so stylish today, even if it was a hand-me-down suit. Her shiny blond hair was neatly arranged beneath a matching mauve hat. The wire-rimmed dark glasses concealed her disability, but her natural beauty still radiated. Allison could tell Lola was impressed by Heather's appearance.

"Are you hungry, Heather?" Allison asked, anxious to get her away from Lola's prying eyes. "We could go track down the diner."

"Yes, I feel like I could eat a horse. Would you care to join us, Miss Stevens?"

Allison winced. Why did Heather have to invite Lola? Fortunately, Lola declined. Allison grabbed Heather's arm and whisked her off to the front of the train.

"Allison, this is such fun," Heather giggled. "I do feel sort of guilty, though, because I don't even miss Grace and the boys yet."

"Don't worry, Heather. It'll come."

Once seated at a table, Allison read the menu to Heather

and they both picked the Pioneer Special.

Allison leaned over and asked, "Do you think Lola suspects anything, Heather?"

"What do you mean?"

"Well, she was looking at you real hard, and I wondered if your dark glasses tipped her off to your being blind."

"But don't people in Hollywood wear dark glasses all the time?" Heather asked with a puzzled brow. "That's what Grace said. She said they make me look very fashionable." Heather giggled. "Of course, she probably just wanted to make me feel better. You know how sweet Grace is. . . ."

"Oh no, Heather. Grace was telling the truth. They do make you look quite chic. Maybe Lola doesn't suspect a thing. She was probably just admiring your suit."

Heather smiled. "My pre-war hand-me-down?"

"Sure. It looks great. But tell me, Heather, why in the world did you invite Lola to join us in the diner?"

"Allison, it would've been terribly rude not to," Heather scolded.

"Look, Heather, we don't have to include her in anything. She's the enemy—remember?"

Heather stroked her water glass with her fingertips, lightly tracing the train's embossed gold symbol. "Allison, Lola is just doing her job."

Allison scowled. She knew she was being unreasonable, but she wanted Heather to hate Lola as much as she did. "Heather, Lola is trying to take me away from Dad—"

"I know," Heather said softly. "But she's still a person. Why don't you try to be nicer to her."

Allison didn't want to be nice to Lola, and she was getting tired of Heather harping on it. The waiter brought their lunch, and Allison mechanically relayed the arrangement on Heather's plate the way she'd heard Grace do. "Tea to your upper right, Salisbury steak at six o'clock, peas at three, and a slippery pear with grated cheese at nine—no, make that ten."

Heather smiled. "Thanks, Al."

When Allison heard the familiar nickname, it melted her heart. "I'm sorry I snapped at you, Heather. Maybe you're right about Lola, but old habits are hard to break."

The girls spent the rest of the day out of Lola's sight, exploring the train and spying on people—Allison would describe the passengers, and Heather would make up crazy stories about each of them. Lola didn't seem to notice or mind that the girls kept their distance. She checked on them at bedtime to see that they were in their sleeper.

"Good night, Lola dear," Allison sang out sarcastically. Lola grunted and banged the door shut.

"Oh, Al!" Heather exclaimed in mock disgust.

"All I said was 'good night.'"

Heather sighed from the lower bunk and changed the subject. "Don't you just love the feel of trains at night?" she asked. "It reminds me of England when my mum used to take us to the country to escape the London heat in summer. We'd ride all night up to Scotland, then stay at this little inn by a lake. It was wonderful. I can't remember if Winston ever got to go, but he'd have been too tiny to remember, anyway. Andrew and I had such fun playing in the cold mountain lake. Come to think of it, that's where I first learned to swim. You know what's really odd, Al— my mum was a lot like Grace. She always wanted me to do the same things other children did. Daddy tried to protect me, but Mum would say, 'No, Jackson, she must learn to do for herself.' It's amazing how God sent Grace to us at just the right time— don't you think so, Al?"

"Yes, I kind of feel like that, too."

"Do you think your father will propose to her?"

"That would be wonderful, but I hope they don't rush into anything. They probably need to get to know each other again. . . ." A small wave of jealousy hit Allison. She had just found her father. She wasn't ready to share him with anyone right away, not even Grace.

"Tell me about your mum, Al."

"Marsha? Hmm . . . what's to tell? I hardly even know her myself. She's considered to be very beautiful. Does that mean anything to you—I mean, since you can't see?"

Heather laughed. "Of course, silly. Like when I smell a rose, I know it's beautiful. Or the sound of the ocean, or the feeling I get when someone I love hugs me. And I think you and Grace are beautiful, too, Al."

Allison snickered. "Well, you probably wouldn't understand how anyone could think Marsha was beautiful. She may be attractive, but it's more like a marble statue. Nicely sculpted but cold and hard. Personally, I don't even think she's that good-looking. She's certainly not as pretty as you are, Heather."

Heather laughed again. "Al, you're sweet—but silly."

"No, Heather, I mean it. You are incredibly pretty. I even saw Lola watching you and I know she was impressed, and she's around actresses and movie stars all the time—"

"Well, Allison, according to Andrew, you're quite a knockout yourself."

Allison leaned over the top bunk and threw her pillow at Heather, instigating an impromptu pillow fight. But Heather soon gained the advantage in the darkened sleeping car, and the battle ended in hysterical giggles.

&c &c &c

The next morning Heather nudged Allison. "Come on,

sleepyhead. I'm starved." Heather was already dressed with her hair neatly arranged.

Allison pushed herself up on one elbow and looked around groggily. She let Heather pull her out of bed, and she grabbed her clothes out of her suitcase. "How do you do your hair so nicely?" Allison asked as she buttoned her seersucker blouse.

"Grace taught me how. It's really quite simple. I'll show you later. I think yours is long enough to do it, too."

When Allison was ready, the girls made their way to the dining car. It was still early and the tables were all but empty. They sat by the window, and Allison admired the craggy mountainous landscape.

"We must be in the Rocky Mountains, Heather."

"That's right, ladies," the waiter said brightly. "We just crossed into Wyoming." He took their order, and Allison tried to describe the majesty of the mountainside landscape.

"It's kind of like God was in this wildly creative mood, and He took all this clay and rock and some scrubby trees. Then He stacked and piled them until they reached way up into the sky. . . ."

Heather laughed. "It sounds very interesting. When do you suppose we'll get to the camp, Al? I think I'm already starting to get homesick. I'd like to write a letter, but my typewriter is still in baggage."

"We'll write post cards right after breakfast. You can dictate to me if you want, Heather, and I'll just write, I won't even listen."

Heather chuckled. "As if I'd have anything to say that you wouldn't know. But on the other hand, do I get to hear what you write to my brother?"

"Heather!" Allison exclaimed in mock irritation.

They finished breakfast, and Allison kept a lookout for Lola in hopes of avoiding her. Heather dictated only one letter and Allison tucked in her own footnotes. By afternoon, they began crossing the Great Plains. Allison told Heather about the circus train that had derailed near Omaha on her trip west.

"You mean giraffes and elephants were actually roaming around on the prairie?" Heather laughed.

"Yes, even monkeys hanging on the train signals—"

"Hello, girls," Lola interrupted as she approached them. "I'm glad to see someone is enjoying this trip." Her voice, as usual, sounded exasperated with life in general.

"We're having a super time, Miss Stevens," Heather said. "Would you like to join us? Al was just telling the funniest story."

"I can just imagine." Lola peered at Allison over her glasses. "Allison, dear, where on earth did you get that lovely suit? It looks just like a Vanderpool."

Allison looked down at the celery-colored linen suit she'd taken from Marsha's closet. "Now that you mention it, Lola, I was wondering the same thing about what you had on yesterday. I think we must shop at the same store."

Lola's face grew red as she pursed her lips and looked out the window.

"Miss Stevens, are you having a nice trip?" Heather asked pleasantly.

Lola grunted. "Humph, I don't know how anyone can sleep on this rickety old train, and the food is disgusting—"

"I'm so sorry," Heather said. "You must be anxious to get home."

"No, not really—it's hotter than an oven in New York this time of year. But at least next week I fly out to Beverly Hills. Somehow summer's more bearable where they have pools and air conditioning."

"And what will you be doing there, Miss Stevens?"

"You might as well call me Lola. That's all right with me. Anyway, Allison's mother will be signing a new contract this fall, and I'm assisting in negotiations and things. You see, Marcus Hudson is Marsha's agent, but he can't be completely trusted, so Marsha has me keep tabs on things."

Allison marveled at Heather's ability to get Lola to talk. In fact, Lola actually seemed to begin to enjoy herself. Most of it was idle chatter or Hollywood gossip, but it did help pass the time. When Lola's tongue finally grew tired, she turned the conversation around. "Heather, I'm curious—you're obviously from England. How did you end up in Oregon of all places?"

Heather explained how her parents were killed in a London blitz and how Grace had adopted the three children. "I love living in Oregon. I think Tamaqua Point is one of the most wonderful spots on the whole coast."

"I suppose it's okay if you like the wilds." Lola turned up her nose. "I prefer a little more civilization. Speaking of which, I'm simply craving a cigarette. I think I better find the smoking car. Maybe I'll join you girls for dinner."

"That would be lovely," Heather said, and Allison wanted to smack her.

"That would be lovely," Allison mimicked when Lola was out of sight.

"Gee, Al, you've got the old Brit accent down just about right," Heather teased. "Come on, Allison, be a sport. Poor Lola isn't having much fun as it is."

Allison reluctantly went to find a table in the dining car with room enough for three. She and Heather eagerly pored over the menu, and Allison secretly hoped Lola had become lost somewhere in the caboose. They waited almost twenty minutes before Lola joined them in the crowded dining car.

"Sorry, have you been waiting long?"

"It's okay," Heather replied. "It gave us time to make up our minds. We're trying the teriyaki tonight."

"Hmm," Lola browsed the menu. "That sounds exotic."

When they had ordered, Lola turned to Allison. "Was it worth it? Running away, I mean."

"Actually, Lola, it was. And it was the only way I ever would have met my grandfather, not to mention discover that Dad was alive."

"That certainly threw me for a loop! I thought James had died in the war. I always kind of liked him, and I never did understand why Marsha—" she checked herself. "I just don't know why their marriage didn't work. Of course, your grandmother Madison was against it from the start." Lola lit a cigarette and blew out a long puff of blue smoke. "But he's still just as handsome as ever. I wonder what Marsha will think. . . ?"

"How long will she and Stanley be in Istanbul?" Allison asked.

"A few more weeks at the very least. They've run into some snags. Ever since the war, life's gotten a lot more complicated over there. Why anyone would want to shoot on location in Istanbul beats me."

"I think it sounds terribly interesting," Heather said.

"Only if you like dirt and flies. I'm just glad I didn't have to go. Thank goodness for Stanley. I sure hope this doesn't ruin their marriage." Lola laughed.

It was dark outside now, and Allison observed their images reflected in the dining car's large plate-glass window. She could still see the faint outline of landscape whizzing by; a lone cow, an occasional tree or fence post. Lola pulled out a tube of lipstick and a little mirror, and Allison watched her reflection in the window as she expertly painted her lips dark red. Lola wasn't unattractive, but her face was long and her nose narrow.

She wore too much makeup, giving her an even harsher look.

"Heather," Lola scolded. "For heavens sake, take off your sunglasses. How can you even see? The sun went down ages ago."

Heather laughed and removed the dark green glasses. Her pale eyes were pretty, but there was a blankness to them.

"Heather, you're an extremely nice-looking girl. Have you ever considered an acting career? I believe you'd have a very photogenic face." Lola reached across the table and tilted Heather's chin to the right and nodded in approval.

Heather giggled nervously. "Thank you, but I doubt very much they use blind girls in movies."

Lola's hand dropped and she stared into Heather's eyes. "My goodness, you're not joking, are you?"

Heather shook her head. "I could just imagine myself tripping over the scenery and knocking into cameras. If I was supposed to kiss the leading man, I might kiss the horse instead." Allison burst into laughter at Heather's description, and even Lola had trouble hiding a smile.

"Does this camp know about your handicap?" Lola asked in a serious tone.

"Well, no . . ."

"But then neither did you, Lola," Allison pointed out. "At least not until now."

Three

"I CAN'T BELIEVE we're almost there!" Heather exclaimed. Allison watched anxiously for road signs as they sat in the backseat of the hired car.

"I can't believe I let your father talk me into this," Lola said from the front. "This place is out in the middle of nowhere!" She turned to the driver. "Are you sure you're not lost?"

"I told you already, ma'am, I know this area like the back of my hand." He pulled his cap down over his forehead and mumbled to himself about city women.

"There's the sign, Lola!" Allison blurted out. "Lakeview Christian Camp, one mile!" The driver turned down the dusty gravel road and sighed in relief.

"Now, Allison, remember," Lola began in a hushed voice. "I won't take any responsibility for Heather's . . . uh . . . well, you know what I mean!"

"I know, Lola, we've got everything under control. Just relax."

They pulled up to an immense building constructed entirely of logs. A tall wooden flagpole stood in front. "This is it," the driver proclaimed proudly, as if they hadn't noticed. He unloaded their bags and waited for Lola.

"You're sure your father took care of everything, Allison? Do I need to sign anything?"

"No, Lola, you've got all the information in that envelope, and Dad wired money for our fees. Don't worry, you're rid of us at last." Allison couldn't hide her sarcasm.

Lola frowned with uncertainty. "Well, you girls have fun, now." She shifted her purse from one hand to the next. "And drop me a card—let me know how things turn out."

"We will, Lola. Thanks for everything," Heather said politely. Allison watched the car drive away in a cloud of dust, then turned and squinted up at the lodge.

"Hello, new campers!" A large, buxom woman in khaki shorts clumped down the front steps. "You must be Allison and Heather. I've been expecting you. I'm Miss Campbell, the assistant director." She slapped them both on the back. "Well, you've missed half the season, but I hope you'll enjoy the rest. You're lucky you had John Stewart in there pitching for you, 'cause we don't usually take in stragglers like this. Of course, even God has mercy on latecomers." She laughed at her own joke and slapped them on the back again. "Hey, Monica!" she yelled across the grassy green knoll that led down to the lake.

A tall brunette who appeared to be their age looked over and ran up the hill toward them. "Yes?" Monica stood before Miss Campbell almost at attention, then glanced at Allison and scowled.

"Monica, please show our new campers to their quarters." Miss Campbell turned back to the girls. "As you know, the boys' camp is on the other side of the lake. Their grounds are strictly off limits. We do share the same mess facilities, but boys are seated in the north hall and girls in the south. Fraternizing is allowed during free times, but you'll find that there are precious little of those. We will keep you busy around here."

Suddenly, Allison felt herself standing at attention like Monica. "Yes, ma'am," she answered as if she were now in the army. "We're looking forward to it."

"And pick up some supplies and uniforms on your way," Miss Campbell added to Monica.

Allison looked at their pile of luggage. "Should we take these, too?" she asked. Miss Campbell nodded and went back up the steps. As she tried to gather her bags, Allison looked down at her high heels. *Not exactly hiking material*, she thought. Heather's weren't much better. Hopefully they didn't have far to go.

"Heather," Allison suggested, "let's just take a few things now, then come back for the rest after we change." She glanced at Monica. "Is that okay?"

Monica shrugged and took off up the hill behind the lodge. Allison grabbed Heather's hand and followed along the dirt trail. They tripped and stumbled behind Monica until they came to a smaller log building. Monica went inside as they dropped their bags and gasped for air.

"Here, I hope these fit." Monica shoved khaki uniforms at them. She piled on blankets, pillows, and other household supplies.

"We can't begin to carry all this stuff," Allison said.

"It's okay. You can make more trips." Monica took a mop and a bucket and headed on up the hill.

"Heather," Allison whispered. "You wait here, and I'll come back and take you up slowly." Allison dashed after Monica, who seemed part mountain goat, and they climbed and climbed. They passed a number of small log cabins along the way but continued on upward.

"Say, Monica," Allison puffed. "Where is this place, anyway—top of the world?"

"Almost," Monica answered. "But when you come late like this, it's the best we can do."

Allison's heel caught on a root and she tripped for the umpteenth time. She set her suitcase by the path and removed her jacket, which was covered in trail dust and debris. She laid it on her suitcase to pick up later, then continued on.

At last they came to a forlorn cabin high up on the hill. It looked like it had been abandoned for years. Monica opened the squeaky door and tossed her scanty load on the grimy floor, then turned to leave.

"Is this where we're supposed to stay?" Allison exclaimed in disbelief as she stared at the shabby cabin. The screens were coated with dust, the floorboards were uneven, and the bunkbeds looked as if they hadn't been slept in for years, at least not by humans.

"That's right. Welcome to Spruce Cabin," Monica said.

"Looks more like Sparse Cabin." Allison groaned.

"At least you have a nice view."

Allison turned around and followed Monica's gaze. She was amazed at the view before her. The lake shimmered below like a sparkling sapphire framed in green trees. From up here, the camp looked spectacular. "It is beautiful, but Spruce Cabin could use a little sprucing up, don't you think?"

"That's what the broom and mop are for. You see, no one's used this cabin since—" Monica got a peculiar look in her eye.

"Since what?"

"Oh, nothing really. It's just some people think this cabin is haunted, but you don't believe in ghosts, do you?"

"No, I guess not." Allison looked over her shoulder warily.

"It's just nonsense. Don't let it bother you. By the way, you're Allison O'Brian, aren't you?"

"How did you know?" Allison couldn't remember any introductions.

"John Stewart mentioned you when camp started. He was really worried about this redhead he'd met on the train. When he heard you were coming he was thrilled." Monica turned on her heel and disappeared down the trail.

Allison quickly unloaded what few belongings she had managed to carry up the hill. She slipped on her loafers and headed back down to fetch Heather.

"I was starting to wonder if I'd been abandoned," Heather called as Allison plodded down the trail.

"I'm sorry, Heather. It's quite a hike. Do you have some sturdier shoes in that bag?"

After Allison slowly led Heather up the hill, she situated her with the layout of the cabin, then they both changed clothes and Allison dashed back down the hill to bring up the rest of their gear. It took two more trips before she was able to dump the last load in their cabin. She collapsed on the bed and wondered if her legs would ever function again.

"I'm sorry, Allison. I'm not much help, am I?"

Allison glanced around the room and noticed the neatly made bunks and the swept floor. Even the pine needles were gone. "Well, it looks like you've been busy, too. It actually looks better in here."

"I beat the mattresses before I made the beds. I swept the floor as best I could, but it still feels gritty."

"It sure is an improvement. We'll need to find some water to scrub this floor—it's disgusting. And if we're going to spend several weeks here we can at least start out clean." Allison got her second wind and located a pump next to an ancient-looking outhouse. Allison swept down cobwebs while Heather scrubbed screens, and before long the cabin was almost homey. In the supply bundle, Allison found a small ball of clothesline and strung it between the cabin and outhouse.

"Heather, just follow this line when you need to visit the facilities. I'll string up a couple more so you can go out from the cabin a ways. You'll have to be really careful because there are some drop-offs nearby. If you want to go anywhere else, we'll have to go together."

"I hope I'm not going to bog you down—"

"Heather Amberwell, don't you dare think that! I'm just thankful you came. In fact, I like this little cabin up here. It's kind of like we're all alone in the wilderness. And the view is fantastic. The lake looks like a bright blue jewel down there, and the sky is so close you can almost reach out and touch it."

"I like it, too. It reminds me of when we used to go to Scotland. Even the air smells kind of like that. . . ." The faint sound of a bell ringing below drifted up the hillside, interrupting their quiet moment.

Allison looked at her watch. "That must be the dinner bell. It's a good thing, too. I've never been so hungry in my life!"

Allison tied a piece of clothesline to the back of her belt for Heather to hold as they went down the hill. She took it slow and easy and wondered how it would feel to be in Heather's place.

In the mess hall, everyone was standing with bowed heads while Miss Campbell prayed. Her long-winded blessing gave the girls plenty of time to slip in unnoticed before she proclaimed a hearty amen. They sat by themselves at a corner table and ate hungrily.

"At least the food is good," Allison commented as she took a bite of tender roast beef.

"Yes, it'd be tasty even if we weren't starving."

"You know, Heather, I've got this funny feeling about that Monica. I don't think she likes me very much."

"Allison, you're awfully suspicious! Monica seemed like a nice enough girl to me. You just haven't given her much of a chance."

"Good evening, ladies, and welcome to Lakeview." John

Stewart stood next to their table and looked at Allison. His eyes were just as blue as she remembered.

"John Stewart, it's you! Can you believe this? We're really here!"

He grasped her hand and shook it warmly. "And who's your friend?" He looked at Heather, and as if on cue she turned her head away.

"This is Heather. She's kind of shy." Allison gently jabbed Heather with her elbow. This was their plan when Heather went without sunglasses in the evening. She'd play the part of the shy friend. John looked back to Allison.

"Where are you staying?"

"Spruce Cabin."

"Spruce Cabin? You're kidding! They put you way up there?" Allison nodded and John scratched his head. "That's weird."

"It's okay, John. We cleaned it up and we like it. It has a beautiful view."

"Has anyone filled you in on the schedule yet?"

"Well, not really, but we only just got here."

"I probably won't see much of you ladies. I'm head counselor for the younger teens, and I've got a bunch of boys who really keep me on my toes. Last night they put a big snake in the girls' shower room. Don't tell, though. No one knows who did it." He winked knowingly.

After dinner, Allison and Heather walked down to the lake. The other campers returned to their cabins to prepare for the evening campfire, but the girls decided to avoid the long hike back up and then down again. Instead, they sat on the dock and Allison described the lay of the camp to Heather.

"There's a boathouse on the east side of the lake and a long, narrow dock with about twenty rowboats and canoes tied to it. Over to the west looks like a sports area, with nets and ball diamonds and whatnot. Then there's a roped-off swim area just to our left with a floating dock. The shore looks nice and sandy with lots of inner tubes strewn about, and there's a long rope swing tied to a tree branch that extends out over the water—it looks like fun."

"Sounds swell. I can't wait for tomorrow, but right now I sure miss Grace and the boys."

"I know how you feel. Even though I only got to spend a couple of days with my dad, I really miss him. And Grandpa, too."

Heather reached for Allison's hand. "I understand what it's like to lose someone you love. Some of those feelings never go away . . . they just get easier."

The bell rang again and this time it sounded much louder. They heard laughs and hoots from other kids as they poured from their cabins. Allison noticed they wore sweaters and sweat shirts and carried flashlights. It was getting cooler now and a breeze stirred, making small dimples in the lake.

"You know, Heather, we don't even have a flashlight to find our way back when it gets dark. I don't know about you, but I might get us lost."

Heather laughed. "A flashlight won't do me much good, but I'm not very familiar with the trail, either. I'm so tired I wouldn't mind just returning to our cabin for the night. Do you think anyone would notice or care?"

"Not if they don't see us. Besides that, it's getting cold and we didn't bring sweaters. We'll come better prepared tomorrow night."

Allison made sure no one noticed as they slowly wound their way up the hill. The climb seemed a tiny bit shorter this time.

"After a few more trips, I just might figure this trail out," Heather said with confidence.

"You're kidding! How?"

"Mostly by counting, timing, and just getting the feel of it— it's hard to explain."

The sunset filled Spruce Cabin with a warm, rosy glow, giving it an air of rustic charm. It seemed to welcome them home, like an old friend that had been rescued from a life of destitution.

"Guess what color the sky is right now?" Allison asked.

"Pink," Heather answered without missing a beat. They laughed and stepped inside just as a gray squirrel scurried across the floor and out the open door.

"What's that?" Heather squealed, clutching Allison's arm.

"Just a cute little squirrel that's probably been living here all summer. I hope he doesn't mind being evicted."

"I hope he didn't discover Muriel's box of treats."

"That's right!" Allison exclaimed. "That walk made me hungry again—how about you?" She fiddled with the kerosene lantern until she finally got it to work. It cast a friendly radiance across the room. They slipped into their flannel nighties and ate coconut macaroons and chocolate fudge on Heather's bed.

"You know, Heather," Allison said mysteriously. "Monica said Spruce Cabin is reputed to be haunted."

"Really? How exciting! Did she say how?"

"No, but we could make something up. Let's see . . ." Allison began her story in a serious tone. "It all happened a few years back, on a cool summer night just like this. Some girls about our age were staying in this very cabin. One of them, a particularly greedy girl named Henrietta Buford, had this insatiable sweet tooth, and she liked to steal goodies from her friends. So one dark night she slipped away from the campfire and sneaked back to the cabin before her friends."

Allison lowered her voice to a near whisper, sending goosebumps along the girls' arms. "Henrietta went through everyone's favorite hiding spots but couldn't find anything to eat except a mushy apple and a stale sandwich. After a long search, she found a gigantic box hidden under her best friend's bed. It was full of chocolate fudge—Henrietta's favorite. She ate and ate—until the last piece of fudge was gone. Then Henrietta—" Allison paused and the cabin grew deathly silent. "Blew up!" she screamed.

Heather leaped from the bed in fright. "Allison O'Brian! You're awful!"

"I'm sorry," Allison choked, collapsing on the bed in a fit of giggles.

"And I suppose you think I'm Henrietta—and I'm going to eat your fudge!"

"No, not at all, Heather. I was just being silly. But now that you mention it, I am partial to fudge."

"Well, that's good, because I'm partial to macaroons!" Heather laughed.

Allison blew out the light and they climbed into bed. It was blacker than ink, but after a while Allison's eyes adjusted until she could see outside. The sky was dark. Allison figured clouds must be blocking the moon and stars. The pine-scented breeze filtered fresh and clean through the screen windows, masking the musty smell of the cabin. Allison pulled the wool blanket up to her chin. "Are you warm enough, Heather?" she asked.

"I'm fine, thanks. Good night, Al."

"Good night, Heather." An owl hooted outside and the wind whistled through the trees. Allison got an idea. She crooned in a scary voice, "I've come . . . I've come . . . I've come for my fudge. Ooo—"

"Shut up, Henrietta!" Heather laughed.

Four

ALLISON LAY WIDE AWAKE in bed. The haunting sound of the wind on the mountain filled her with a sense of melancholy. She thought about her father and how sad his eyes looked when they'd said good-bye. She wondered how long it would be until she was with him again. And what would Marsha say about all this? She had to let Allison stay in Oregon. She just had to.

Suddenly, Allison heard a loud scratching noise, and her worries over Marsha were instantly replaced with fear. Was it a wild animal out in the woods? She'd read a story once about a bear attack, and the memory of it sent shivers down her spine. Even if they screamed at the top of their lungs, who would ever hear them way up here?

"Allison," Heather whispered. "Are you still awake?"

"Uh-huh."

"I can't sleep, Allison. I've never stayed in the woods like this and I don't mean to be a baby, but I feel kind of . . . well, sort of—"

"Scared." Allison finished her sentence. "Me too. I've only been to a camp where you stay with lots of other girls and much closer to camp. This feels kind of strange to me."

"Sometimes when I'm frightened, Grace and I pray together. We could do that," Heather suggested. Allison scrambled down from the upper bunk and got into bed with Heather.

"Dear God," Heather prayed. "We're scared. It feels lonely up here, but I know you're close by. You love us and want to take care of us. So please, help us not to be so afraid."

Allison immediately felt as if a load had been lifted.

"Would you mind if I played my flute?" Heather asked.

"Oh, I wish you would!"

Heather scooted her flute case from beneath her bed and soon sweet, fluid notes drifted through the cabin. Allison laid her head back on Heather's pillow and let the soothing music carry her away. It sounded like sunshine, and it reminded her of the little sandpipers that raced along the wet beaches in Oregon. Suddenly, Heather stopped in the middle of a stanza.

"I hear something," Heather whispered. Allison sat up to listen but could hear nothing. They sat frozen, listening to the sounds of the woods until Allison thought she heard something, too. Heather clutched Allison's arm as the sound grew closer. A loud tramping and rustling of bushes came right up to the cabin, then the door flew open and a flashlight glared into the room. Allison stared as three dark shadows lurked in the doorway. Her heart pounded in her eardrums, but she felt too frightened to move. She was sure Heather's grip on her arm would break it in two.

"Thank goodness you're here," John Stewart exclaimed breathlessly.

"Land sakes, that's an awful hike!" an older male voice gasped. "I'm sorry to frighten you girls. I'm Len Stanton, the camp director. John was worried about you two when you didn't show up for the campfire. And when he mentioned you'd been put in the Spruce Cabin, I became concerned, too. We don't use this cabin anymore—it's too far removed from the rest of the camp."

Allison found her voice. "You mean not because it's haunted?"

Len chuckled. "Haunted? Not likely." He turned to Monica,

who stood sheepishly behind John. "Did you tell these girls it was haunted?"

She hung her head and nodded.

"You mean we weren't really supposed to stay here in the first place?" Heather asked. "After we cleaned it and everything?"

"I'm so sorry, girls," Len said. "Monica, we should make you stay up here all by yourself! That'd teach you a lesson."

"Actually, we kind of liked it," Allison told him. "At least until nighttime. Of course, the hike is something else. . . . Oh no, does this mean we have to haul everything back down again?"

"No, Monica will take care of that tomorrow," Len said in a voice of authority. "You can either spend the night up here and Monica will keep you company, or you can come down and stay in a much nicer cabin. It's your decision."

"What do you think, Heather?" Allison asked.

"I don't mind staying here for the night," Heather said. Monica groaned.

"Then it's settled," Allison announced, glad to see Monica squirming. "In fact, we were just starting to enjoy it—before you frightened us, that is."

"We heard that beautiful flute music," John said. "Who plays?"

"That's Heather," Allison said proudly.

"Heather, I don't suppose I could entice you to share your music at campfire with us?" Len asked.

"Sure, I'd love to."

"Great! Now, you're certain you'll be okay? Monica brought her sleeping bag, and I'm sure she'll love spending the night up here." Len chuckled as he and John departed.

"Are you sure you don't want to return with them?" Monica asked hopefully.

"No, we're fine," Allison answered, climbing back into her bunk. She heard Monica sigh in exasperation as she threw her bag onto the bunk across the room, and she bit her lip to keep from laughing out loud.

⚭   ⚭   ⚭

The next morning, Allison awoke to chirping birds and sunshine streaming through her window. She stretched and breathed deeply the fresh air, then looked over to see Monica twisted in her sleeping bag with a sour expression on her face. Heather was already up and dressed.

"Thank heavens it's morning," Monica groaned. "I didn't sleep a wink all night."

Monica was all too eager to help them pack up their things and make their way back to camp. She grumbled as she led the way down the trail, practically shoving them into the nice bathroom facility at the foot of the hill. They enjoyed hot showers and the luxury of real plumbing.

Following a hearty breakfast, Monica showed them to Oak Cabin and, according to Len's commands, carried all their suitcases for them, dumping them with a loud grunt when she finished.

Their new cabin was squeaky clean and situated near the lake. It had shiny glass windows instead of screens. They met their cabin mates and unpacked their bags for the second time. Then everyone pitched in to clean the already spotless cabin.

"We do this every morning," one girl explained. "We have the record for the cleanest cabin in camp, and we want to win the award at the end of the season. So even though it looks clean, we try to make it better." Allison and Heather helped straighten the white stones that led up the immaculate walk to the cabin.

A young woman with sleek black hair that was pulled back into a long ponytail approached them. "Hi, I'm Constance, and I'm your counselor. I hear you girls had quite a first day. You'll have to excuse Monica. She's Miss Campbell's niece and gets a little carried away sometimes. I see the girls have already put you to work. I'm managing the boathouse today, so come by and say hi later during sports time.

"I'll give you both a schedule at lunch. Until then, your cabin mates can help you find your way around. We allow our campers a certain amount of independence, but we expect you to be responsible, too. Some activities are optional, but Chapel, Bible class, and the evening campfire are mandatory. I'm sure you both will fit right in." Constance smiled warmly.

Another girl with short chestnut hair and a golden tan welcomed them. "Hi, my name's Barbara. Our cabin is signed up for the craft shed this morning, but first we have Chapel. You gals coming?"

"Sure, sounds swell," Allison answered.

Chapel was held under the trees and led by Pastor Warren, who lived in the nearby town. Allison tried her best to listen to his words, but her eyelids drooped heavily. Her long night in Spruce Cabin was definitely taking its toll. At last Pastor Warren said amen, and the campers scurried back out into the sunshine.

At the craft shed they worked on clay pottery and took turns on the two kick wheels. Allison watched Heather expertly maneuver the slippery clay on the spinning wheel, then glanced back at her own lopsided pot. "Heather, you must have done this before!" she exclaimed.

Heather laughed and nodded, giving the wheel another firm kick. "We had potters' wheels like these at Tamaqua Junior

High. I always liked making pots." The others gathered and looked on with admiration. Heather's head bent low over her work and her long golden braid trailed down her back. No one noticed her eyes.

Barbara told them that they were scheduled for water sports next. After a few water relays, they were allowed to swim freely until lunch. Allison stayed close to Heather, and they laughed and splashed together, holding hands to jump off the dock. Allison had devised a series of code words to direct Heather without alerting the other girls to her blindness. It had become a game of sorts and they were getting good at it, but Allison worried about what might happen if their secret was uncovered. She couldn't bear to see Heather sent home.

Allison and Heather climbed out of the lake and flopped down on the warm, sandy beach to dry in the sun. "Oh, Al, this is such fun. I can't wait to tell everyone at home what a great time we're having. I suppose I better not pull out my typewriter just yet. That might look suspicious."

"That's okay. I'll write letters for both of us." Allison glanced hesitantly at her friend. "Heather, how are you doing with all this? Does being away from home make you nervous?"

"A little bit. But mostly I feel guilty, like we're deceiving everyone here. Do you think it's wrong?"

Allison picked up a handful of sand and watched as it slipped through her fingers. She thought for a moment before answering. "I think it's wrong for you to be excluded just because you can't see. You have just as much business being here as I do. I just wish we didn't have to sneak around so much."

"What are you two whispering about?" Barbara asked, dropping down beside them in a soggy heap. "Some deep, dark secrets I suppose—or just boys?"

"We were just discussing a friend of ours," Heather said

mysteriously. "Her name was Henrietta and she died a tragic death." Both girls burst into laughter.

"Really? What happened?" Barbara's eyes widened in surprise.

"Allison will have to tell you all later on tonight . . . when it's dark," Heather whispered.

Later that afternoon, they had two hours of free time. They visited with Constance at the boathouse for a while, then took out a sleek blue canoe. Allison rowed them to the middle, then pulled in the paddle. There in the center of the sparkling lake, Heather played her flute while Allison wrote letters to home.

"Be sure and tell Andrew that John Stewart still thinks you're pretty special," Heather teased.

"What makes you think I'm writing to Andrew?"

"Well, who are you writing to?"

Allison didn't answer.

"I knew it!" Heather exclaimed. "I could tell because you were so quiet."

"Heather, sometimes you can be very irritating!" Allison laughed as she slipped Andrew's letter safely into an envelope. "Besides, that's not true about John. He's just a good friend and you know it!"

"Well, Monica didn't think so, did she?"

"So you admit it, Heather. I was right about Monica, wasn't I?"

"I suppose so, Al." Heather's head drooped. "I guess sometimes I can be pretty gullible. . . . Andrew is always warning me about—"

"Oh, Heather, that's what I love about you—and it's not that you're gullible. It's just that you always think the best of people, and that's nice. You were right about Lola. I mean . . . she's not all bad. But don't forget Shirley, who didn't care if you drowned as long as she didn't get her hair wet!"

"Of course!" Heather giggled. "But dear, brave Allison was there to save me!" They both laughed loudly.

"Hey, what's the joke?" Barbara called as she and Sarah, another one of their cabin mates, rowed next to them and splashed playfully.

"Just some funny memories," Heather answered.

"Want to race across the lake?" Sarah asked.

"You're on," Allison squealed.

Heather wasn't used to rowing, and Allison worked doubly hard to finish a close second. After they docked the canoe, they dragged themselves to the cool green grass beneath an enormous maple tree.

The other three girls chatted away like old buddies while Allison stretched back and stared up at the gigantic leaves above her. They looked like brilliant green stars with the sunlight filtering through. She rubbed her stinging palms, still hot from rowing. That burning sensation reminded her of her stormy row to the lighthouse—a memory she'd suppressed. She didn't like to think about how close she'd come to dying out in that storm. She didn't want to face the guilt of any unfinished business with God, either. She'd cried out to Him in fear that day, and now she wondered what she owed Him in return. With all these chapels and Bible lessons, she was getting a little worried. She certainly wasn't about to dedicate her life to the mission field and travel to the darkest depths of Africa.

"And you should've seen Monica's face last night at the campfire when Len told her she might have to spend the night in Spruce Cabin." Sarah laughed, tossing her short blond curls.

"Poor Monica," Heather sighed.

"Poor Monica? I felt sorry for *you* two!" Barbara exclaimed. "Though I must admit I was a little jealous. It sounded pretty exciting to spend the night up there all alone!"

"Not to me," Sarah piped up. "I thought for sure you would be back down by midnight. I know I would've."

"Hey, the Snack Shack's open now," Barbara exclaimed, leaping to her feet. "And I'm just dying for a Dr. Pepper!" She reached down to pull up Heather, but naturally Heather didn't respond. Allison looked quickly at Barbara, but Barbara just stood there with her arm outstretched in front of Heather's face.

"Hey, wake up, sleepyhead," Allison said. She grabbed Heather's arm and pulled her to her feet.

"Oh sorry, guess I was daydreaming. . . ."

"That was a close call," Allison whispered as Barbara walked out the door.

"Sooner or later someone's bound to find out, Allison. Maybe I should lay low for a while."

"But you're here to have a good time, not sit in our cabin all day long. If they find out, they find out. If they want to send you home, they'll have to send me, too."

After dinner, they joined the other girls in readying for the campfire. Everyone fixed their hair, brushed their teeth, put on sweat shirts and jerseys, and dug out flashlights and Bibles. Allison had brought along the white Bible Grandmother Mercury had left her. Heather, of course, didn't have one.

"Don't worry, Heather, I'll share mine." Allison laughed, linking arms with her best friend.

"You guys are as inseparable as peanut butter and jelly!" Monica remarked from behind. "Don't you ever let each other out of sight?"

"Not if we can help it," Allison retorted.

They sang lots of lighthearted songs and the counselors did a funny skit that put the campers in stitches. Then Len stood up behind the fire. The leaping orange flames illuminated his face in a flickering glow. After a few brief announcements, he introduced the evening speaker. "Tonight, Constance Green will share her personal testimony."

Constance stood before the campers and shifted uncomfortably from one foot to the next. Allison felt sorry for her. What must it be like to stand up and speak to all those people?

"Hi. As you know, I'm Constance," she began. Her long black hair cascaded over her shoulders and her dark eyes sparkled in the firelight. "I've never done this before, so bear with me. I guess I'll start my story by saying I don't come from your typical, everyday home. You see, my parents never went to church and my dad—" She paused and took a breath. "He used to be an alcoholic . . . in other words, a drunk. For years I tried to keep it a secret. It was hard, though, because I could never invite friends home, and once in a while my dad would show up at a school function after drinking too much. It was very embarrassing for me." She looked up at the darkening sky and continued.

"Anyway, my brother, Rod, became a Christian in high school, and I thought it was funny because I just figured everyone was a Christian. You know, like if you lived in America, you must be a Christian. But I could see something was different about my brother, and he even got Dad to go to some church meetings with him. And then Dad began to change. He even quit drinking. It was amazing! And while that was really great, I still had a problem." She folded her arms across her chest and looked out across the crowd of listening faces.

"You see, I hated my dad. I know that sounds really awful, but it's true. I hated him for ruining Christmas and birthday parties and embarrassing me in front of my friends." She wiped a tear from her eye and shoved her hands into her shorts pockets, then took a deep breath and stood straighter. "Every time

Rod tried to tell me about God, I wouldn't listen. I didn't want to hear it because I knew if I gave my life to God I'd have to forgive Dad. And I just wasn't ready to do that.

"Well, my dad's a miner, and one day it happened—the thing we fear most in Dunnsville. The mine sirens went off and everyone ran down to see. There'd been a huge explosion and a cave-in. Forty-three miners were trapped inside—my dad with them. In my imagination I saw Dad pinned under a heavy beam, breathing his last breath. Suddenly, I was sorry for how I had treated him. I begged God to help him, to spare him. And then I realized, just like that, the hate was gone—completely gone! It was like it had all been erased, and all I could remember was the good things he'd done. I told God I was sorry and asked Him to spare Dad so I could tell him that I loved him.

"It took thirty-five hours to rescue those men. Seventeen died, but Dad came out with just a broken leg. Since then I've let God direct my life. And, well . . . here I am." Constance held up her arms like she didn't know what more to say, and the campers burst into applause. Len led them in a short prayer, and then they sang a few more songs before returning to their cabins.

"Constance, your story was so encouraging," Sarah said as they prepared for bed.

"Yeah, thanks for sharing it," Barbara agreed.

Allison appreciated Constance's words, too, and wished she could think of something to say, but her tongue felt knotted. She lay in bed and replayed the words she'd heard at the campfire. She knew Constance had done the right thing by forgiving her father, but it hit too close to home when she considered her bitter feelings toward Marsha. How could she feel any different?

Five

ALLISON AWOKE TO QUIET MOANING and blackness and wondered where she was. Someone was thrashing and groaning next to her. Then she remembered she was at camp and was sharing a cabin with several other girls. Sarah's bunk was next to hers, and Allison lay stiffly in her bed unsure of what to do. It seemed hours before Sarah settled down and Allison finally fell back to sleep.

The next thing she knew, sunshine poured in through the windows and the morning bell clanged without mercy. The cabin was unusually quiet and nearly empty.

"Hey, lazybones," Sarah called as she pulled on a sandal. "You ever getting up?"

"Mmm . . . I guess so." Allison rubbed her puffy eyes and stretched lazily. She slipped down from her bunk to discover Heather's neatly made bed. "Wow, it must be late."

"She went to breakfast with Barbara," Sarah said, pulling an orange jersey over her camp uniform. "I think she gave up on you."

Allison yanked on her clothes. "Well, Sarah, if you hadn't kept me awake half the night—" She stopped mid-sentence when she noticed Sarah's troubled brown eyes.

"Did I wake you?" Sarah asked meekly.

"Yeah, but it's okay, Sarah. I was just teasing. Sorry. I didn't mean to hurt your feelings."

"Sometimes I have bad nightmares, but I didn't mean to disturb anyone."

"It's all right. Forget about it. I need to hurry and catch up with Heather." Allison didn't even bother to comb her hair. Allison puzzled over how Heather could hide her blindness from Barbara and get to breakfast without any help. She quickly tied her neckerchief as she dashed for the dining hall with Sarah close by her heels.

"Slow down, Allison. What is it? Are you starving or something?"

Allison entered the dining hall and searched the room for Heather. On the far side of the room, she spotted a long golden braid and hurried over.

"Hi, Heather," Allison said almost breathlessly. "Why didn't you wake me?" She glanced at Barbara curiously and then back to Heather. Several other girls from the cabin were already joining them.

"It's okay, Al. I decided to come with Barbara for breakfast." Monica was sitting next to Barbara and rolled her eyes at Allison. "Allison, take it easy. Can't Heather sit with someone else for a change? What are you two—Siamese twins joined at the hip?" Allison smirked at Monica's sarcastic humor.

"What's going on, Heather?" Allison whispered, scooting in beside her friend.

"I'll tell you later," Heather answered. She felt the table for her fork but didn't pick it up. Just then Miss Campbell stepped forward to lead them in prayer.

After breakfast, Allison dumped their plates and led Heather away from the dining hall and over to the dock.

"Relax, Al," Heather consoled. "It was bound to happen."

"What—what do you mean?"

"Barbara knows."

Allison groaned and threw a stone out into the smooth lake. She watched as the tiny circle became another and another and soon the round ripples spanned to the water's edge.

"I got up this morning," Heather began slowly. "I had to use the bathroom. Everyone was asleep—or so I thought. I got dressed and tried to make my way over alone. You know, I've been counting and everything. Somehow I messed up and turned too soon and ended up in a bush. Barbara was on her way back to the cabin, and she pulled me out. It wasn't hard for her to figure out."

"Oh no, do you think she'll tell?"

Heather didn't answer. Instead, she whirled around and there stood Barbara on the dock behind them.

"No, Allison, I'm not going to tell," Barbara declared. "Anyway, who'd care? But if it's that important to keep this thing a secret, I'm game." Allison sighed and smiled at Barbara.

"See, Allison. I told you not to worry. Thanks, Barbara." Heather smiled. "Actually, it feels good to have someone else know—sort of a relief."

"I can help out, too," Barbara said. "I've never known anyone who's blind. I think it's kind of exciting. But we better get back for cabin cleanup now."

After the ritual cleaning, the girls went to Chapel and then to the craft shack again. This time they attempted to create pine needle baskets.

"This is too meticulous for me," Allison moaned. Her fingers had become sticky from the sap, and the needles in her basket stuck out like a wrinkled porcupine. She looked over at Heather's tiny, neat basket. "Well, you certainly are a crafty person, aren't you? Everything you make turns out just about perfect."

"Yeah, isn't she just sickening!" Monica exclaimed. "Is there anything you can't do, Heather?"

"You'd be surprised, Monica." Heather giggled without looking up.

"Why don't you go on ahead to the archery range, Allison," Barbara suggested with a confidential nod. "We're signed up for the next session. I think I'll stay and see if I can get some pointers from Heather."

"I'll join you," Sarah said. "So far none of the girls in our cabin have beat me at target practice. Are you up for the challenge?"

"Sure, I'll give it a shot," Allison said, laughing at her own pun. "I haven't held a bow for a while . . . not since Camp Wannatonka." Allison filled Sarah in on all the awful details of her old camp as they walked over to the archery range. Some high school girls were still finishing their archery session, so Allison and Sarah sat down on a log bench to wait.

"Monica can be pretty snitty, can't she?" Allison commented.

"You're telling me. She can be a pain in the you-know-what. But her biggest problem is she's boy crazy. Not that I don't like boys, but if you get alone with Monica it's all she talks about."

Allison laughed. "I haven't hardly noticed a boy since we got here—except for John Stewart, and he's just a friend."

"Better watch out for Monica, then. She thinks John's about the best thing since sliced bread!"

"Don't I know it. I suspect that's how we ended up in Spruce Cabin to start with." Allison looked up at the hill behind the lodge where she and Heather had spent their first night, then she thought about Sarah's nightmares the night before. "Do you have those nightmares a lot, Sarah?"

Sarah nodded mutely.

"I sort of understand how that feels, Sarah. My grandpa died recently, and I had these awful dreams the first few nights, but then they went away. . . ."

"I wish mine would go away." Sarah looked down. "But I

don't think they ever will. I've had them for years now."

Allison couldn't imagine what could possibly trouble someone like Sarah. Still, she didn't want to pry. Maybe she should try to change the subject. "Sarah, I've been wanting to tell you that I really like your accent. I can't tell exactly where it's from, but I think it sounds very elegant."

Sarah bit her lip and looked across the gleaming lake where tiny ripples sparkled in the sunlight like hundreds of diamonds. "You have a very good ear, Allison. In fact, you're the first one at camp to notice. It's Czechoslovakian. My mother was American, so I've spoken English since birth, but still it's taken me years to lose that accent. My mother is always correcting my pronunciation."

"That's so interesting, Sarah. So then is your father Czech?"

Sarah nodded with a trace of sadness in her eyes. Just then the older girls finished with the archery range, and Allison and Sarah stepped up to pick out their bows. Sarah expertly held hers and shot the arrow with careful accuracy, very close to the bull's eye. The next two were just as good. Allison shot and felt lucky just to hit the target. Sarah patiently gave Allison some tips, and Allison gradually improved.

"This is fun, Sarah," Allison said. "But you better not give me too much more help, or I just might beat you." She shot once again, coming close to the center.

"Yikes! I guess you're on your own from now on." They practiced until the lunch bell rang, then made their way to the dining hall.

"I'm sorry if I was being nosy earlier, Sarah. I didn't mean to. I just wanted to know more about where you're from. It sounds so interesting."

"I guess some people might call it that."

"It sounds terribly romantic to be half Czechoslovakian.

And I don't know why you'd want to lose the lovely accent. How long has it been since you've been there?" Allison paused. "Surely you weren't there during the war."

Sarah turned and looked at Allison, then slowly nodded.

"Oh," Allison said, the pieces of the puzzle finally coming together. "I guess that couldn't have been much fun."

Sarah shook her head. "No, not much fun." Then she spoke in a very quiet, serious voice. "Have you ever heard of Auschwitz, Allison?"

Allison stared at Sarah and swallowed. "Of course . . . it was a horrible Nazi prison camp—they kept Jewish prisoners there. . . ." Her voice trailed off. "Surely, you weren't—"

Sarah nodded soberly. "I'm not supposed to talk about it, but sometimes I feel like if I don't I'll explode."

"You can talk to me, Sarah." They had reached the area near the cabins, and other campers were clambering about.

"Not now, Allison," said Sarah. "But thank you." They parted ways at the bathroom. Other girls chattered noisily as they got ready for lunch, but Allison washed her hands in silence, trying to absorb all she had just heard.

"Hi, stranger." Allison greeted Heather in the dining hall, trying to sound brighter than she felt. "Is everything going okay?" Heather's sunny smile was answer enough. Allison wanted to tell Heather about Sarah, but she knew by the way that Sarah had spoken that this was something she should keep private.

"Heather played her flute for us," Barbara announced. "Constance made her promise to play at the campfire tonight."

"Ooh." Monica faked a dramatic yawn. "That should be terribly entertaining." Allison glared at her.

"Hello, Allison," John said from behind. "How are you doing? Bet you like Oak Cabin better than Spruce." She turned around, and he handed her some letters. "I'm playing postman today, but from now on you will have to remember to pick up your mail at the main lodge. Looks like you and Heather are pretty popular. Miss Campbell said to let you know there's a parcel for you, too."

Allison grinned. "Thanks so much, John!" She sorted the letters and handed some bulky ones to Heather. "Won't we have fun during free time this afternoon, Heather!"

Heather hugged the letters to her chest. "I can hardly wait!"

"So, is John Stewart your personal delivery boy?" Monica asked sourly.

"No, he's just a thoughtful friend," Allison answered.

After Bible class, Heather and Allison picked up their package at the lodge. It was from Muriel. They slipped off to a secluded clearing in the woods to enjoy their letters and treats. Heather's letters were typed in Braille so she needed no assistance. Allison read the letter from her father first.

Dearest Allison Mercury,

When I watched you pull out of Portland, I felt part of me being torn away. But my major consolation is knowing I shall now fight to win you back. Already my lawyer has given me great hope. He's filed a case in New York, and we're hoping it won't take too long to get a court date. He's sent letters and telegrams to Marsha requesting an out-of-court agreement. So far we've heard nothing, but it's still early.

Allison, I feel like I've been given a new life because of you. I still can't believe it. Sometimes I pinch myself to see if I'm dreaming. Grace has been incredibly understanding. After all I put that poor woman through, I'm surprised she even gives me the time of day. Yes, my dear Allison, we are talking about marriage, but we both agree to do nothing until this dilemma with you is solved. We want everyone happily settled first. Besides, we all need time to get used to each other.

Now for another piece of good news. I met my old high school art teacher. He runs a nice gallery in a large tourist town down the coast and wants to show my work. I have quite a bit, and Andrew helped me haul it from the lighthouse. He's such a nice young man. I've asked him to take over the lighthouse for the summer. He and Winston are learning a lot about boating and fishing, and I'm learning some things about being a dad. Life would be perfect if only you and Heather were back with us. But it will happen soon. . . . I just know it.

> *All my love,*
> *Dad*

"Allison, it sounds like they're having such fun. Does it make you feel kind of jealous?" Heather asked.

"Yes, a little," Allison admitted. "It makes me angry at Marsha, too. It's all her fault, you know. If she hadn't butted in, we'd still be there. Are you sorry you came with me, Heather?"

"Oh no! Not at all. I just miss them, is all."

Heather opened up her flute case and began to play. Allison opened Andrew's letter next. It was a nice, friendly letter, describing all the new events in his life. He also said he missed her in such a way that her heart warmed toward him, and she longed to be there. She imagined rowing across the inlet with him, fishing and crabbing together. These were still new feelings for her, and she wished she had someone to talk to. It didn't seem right to discuss her feelings for Andrew with Heather, his very own sister.

Allison noticed they were surrounded by scores of pretty white daisies, and she carefully constructed a daisy chain crown and placed it on Heather's head, then began one of her own.

"It feels lovely, Allison." Heather gently fingered the dainty flowers and picked up her flute again. "I shall play you a song of gratitude." The graceful notes seemed to blend into the woods and harmonize with the birds. Suddenly, Heather stopped and laid the silver flute in her lap, cocking her head to one side as if she had heard something. As if on cue, the bushes rustled and John Stewart appeared.

"Hello there, ladies," he said. "Sorry to interrupt, but I heard such beautiful woodland music. I thought I'd discovered a hidden fairy glen."

"We're rather clumsy for fairies." Heather laughed.

John stared at Heather as if seeing her for the first time. "Actually, Heather, I was wondering if we could practice a few songs together for the campfire. Len gave me permission to come find you so I could accompany you with my guitar—if you don't mind, that is."

"You play guitar?" Heather asked, oblivious to the look of open admiration she was receiving from John. Allison couldn't blame him as she watched her friend sitting in the soft green grass, her legs curled gracefully under her. Wispy blond curls cascaded around her pretty face, framed by the daisy chain. She really did look like a fairy.

"Do you want to meet me at the dock around four? I'll bring my guitar, and we can see what songs we might have in common." His face grew slightly flushed, and he turned and disappeared as fast as he'd come.

"Heather," Allison whispered. "He really seems to like you—a lot!"

"Oh, silly Al." Heather smiled. "There you go again! Say, isn't it time for the Snack Shack to open? I'm thirsty."

They tucked their letters away and headed back. Allison wondered if her suspicions were right this time or if she was just getting caught up in thoughts of romance because of her feelings for Andrew. Still, the way John looked at Heather was nothing like the way he'd looked at Allison before. It didn't make her jealous, just extremely curious.

Later that afternoon, Allison took a box of stationery along with her as she accompanied Heather down to the dock to meet John. She would use this time to answer her letters. John was already there, picking away on his guitar.

"Just warming up," John said, standing to greet them. Allison settled off to the side, keeping a wary eye on the two as they began to play a song. Soon Allison's attention was absorbed in her writing as she heard them play song after song. Apparently they had a lot of music in common. But they didn't just play; they talked off and on, too.

"What's going on here?" Monica demanded as she sauntered up to them with her hands on her hips. "Concert in the park today? Why didn't anyone post a billboard?" Then she flopped down on her stomach and propped her head on her elbows right between Heather and John. "Are you going to play for us again at the campfire tonight, John? It's been such a long time since we've heard you."

John nodded and adjusted a string on his guitar. He started another song and Heather joined in. Their music was lovely, and the lake seemed a perfect backdrop for their impromptu concert. Barbara and Sarah came along shortly and sat down beside Allison, and before long other campers gathered around in a half circle. When the two finished their piece, the crowd applauded and begged for more. Just then the dinner bell rang.

"You'll have to come to the campfire tonight for more," John said. "Heather, that was swell. I'll see you later." He snapped his guitar case closed and took off.

"Well, it seems little Miss Perfect has enchanted John Stewart," Monica announced loudly enough for other campers to hear. Heather's face reddened and Allison darted to her side. Grasping Heather's hand, she pulled her to her feet.

"Great sound, Heather. Personally, I like jazz better, but you guys are pretty snazzy," Barbara complimented, stepping up to them. "Too bad *some* people can't appreciate good music." This comment was tossed in Monica's direction. Barbara linked arms with Heather and guided her toward the cabin. Allison picked up the flute case and followed with Sarah. She appreciated Barbara's help, but at the same time she longed to have Heather all to herself.

"That Monica is really something else," Sarah whispered to Allison as they walked up the hill.

"Yeah, make sure you tell me when you figure out exactly what!" Allison laughed.

Six

IT CAME AS NO SURPRISE to Allison when Heather and John performed beautifully at the campfire that evening. They all listened to the music, sang some nonsensical songs, and made s'mores with graham crackers and marshmallows and chocolate.

"You know why they call them s'mores, don't you?" Sarah asked. Allison shook her head and licked melted chocolate from her fingertips. "Because you always want some more. S'mores—get it?"

Allison laughed and glanced over at Barbara and Heather. John was talking with enthusiasm to Heather, but her head was down. His interest in her was plain to see, and Allison felt a stab of concern. She wondered how he'd react to Heather's blindness. She certainly didn't want Heather to get hurt.

The counselors put on a crazy skit, and after a quick testimony from a nervous counselor they returned to their cabins. Their nightly pilgrimage reminded Allison of a swarm of fireflies as campers trekked their way along the darkened trails with a multitude of flashlight beams.

❧   ❧   ❧

The next day at breakfast, Monica sat next to Heather with Barbara on the other side. Allison felt skeptical about Monica's intentions and kept a wary eye on her. Monica moved Heather's milk glass closer to her and before Allison could put it back,

Heather reached for the glass, bumped it with her hand, and knocked it across the table.

"Here, Heather," Monica offered, dangling a napkin a few inches in front of Heather's unseeing face. Barbara glared at Monica, snatched the napkin, and angrily blotted the milk. Monica grinned shrewdly.

Allison whisked Heather away after breakfast. "I think you'd better keep your distance from Monica," she whispered as they hurried back to their cabin for clean-up time.

Heather nodded. "I guess we'll have to wait and see what comes of it. Maybe it's just a coincidence."

After Chapel, Heather and Barbara signed up for a class at the craft shack, but Allison and Sarah had signed up to take out a canoe.

"Did I disturb you again last night, Allison?" Sarah asked meekly as she sliced a paddle through the water.

"No, I didn't hear anything."

Sarah sighed. "Well, you must've been too tired because last night I had a bad one. . . ."

"Do you want to talk about it? It might help, you know." Allison noticed that Sarah's fists were clenched so tightly her knuckles had turned white.

"I don't know, Allison. I don't know if anything will help. I think it's hopeless."

"Sarah, I know it must have been horrible. I can't even imagine. But keeping it bottled up inside won't make it any better." Allison frowned thoughtfully. "I've been through some hard things, too. Nothing like what you've been through, but it does help to talk about them."

"I was there for almost two years, Allison." Sarah laid the paddle in her lap and watched Allison's face. She held out her wrist and showed Allison a long, straight white scar. "That was where my number used to be. My mother had it removed as soon as I got out."

"Oh, Sarah." Allison reached out and ran her finger along the slender scar. "I'm so sorry." Allison felt tears building in her eyes.

"It's okay, Allison. Maybe you'd rather not hear—"

"You can say anything you want to me, Sarah. I'm your friend. You can trust me."

"I know. I knew that when I saw you helping Heather—"

"You know about Heather?"

Sarah nodded. "I haven't told anyone."

"Thanks. See, we can trust each other."

Sarah reached down and ran her hand through the water. "My papa owned the biggest department store in Bratislava, Czechoslovakia," she began slowly, lapsing into a more noticeable accent. "It was a very nice store called Feldstein's—that was my name then. . . . We were very wealthy and it seemed we should have been happy, but ever since I can remember we lived in fear. It was like this dark, gloomy cloud constantly hovered over us. My mother was an American, very pretty and modern. And my father, Isaac Feldstein"—Sarah spoke the name proudly—"was tall, dark, and handsome—and Jewish. They met in Paris where they were both buying new fashions for their stores. She worked for a big store in New York then. He offered her more money to come work for him, and like a fairy tale they ended up married."

For a moment, Allison almost forgot the dark side of the story. It sounded so enchanting, almost like a romantic novel.

"One day the men in uniforms came to Papa's store. It was raining out and their coats were all wet and drippy. I was there with Papa that afternoon, waiting for Mother to pick me up. I was sitting on the floor in his big wood-paneled office cutting out some new French paper dolls. The Gestapo men took us both, even though Papa said to leave me—that I was American. I remember being terribly worried that their dripping coats were going to ruin my pretty paper dolls. I had no idea. . . ." Sarah looked away. "I only saw Papa twice after that. Once at the train station and once at Auschwitz. Papa never made it out. Mother only got me released because I'm half American."

Allison shook her head in amazement. "But your name is Miller—"

"Mother married again shortly after I came to New York. She'll never love anyone the way she loved Papa, but he's a nice man. The hardest part for me is Mother won't let me talk about it to anyone. She forbids me to even mention Auschwitz. And I know it's just because she is so afraid. She thinks it could happen again. But it's not like I want to tell the world, Allison. It's just that sometimes it wells up inside me and I think I might blow up."

Allison nodded in sympathy. "I felt like that when Grandpa died—in fact, I did kind of explode."

"Thanks for listening, Allison. It's hard to believe, but I feel better having told you. And I don't think Mother will mind since you don't know anyone in Buffalo anyway." Sarah watched as she trailed her fingers along the water. "You know, Allison, I'm half Jewish. Does that bother you?"

"Of course not! Actually, I envy you having such an interesting heritage. I grew up only knowing half of my family background, and they were generation after generation of boring!"

Sarah laughed but grew serious again. "I always have this fear, Allison. I know this is America and it's supposed to be different here, but I worry that someone will find out that I'm Jewish and hate me."

"I think that's how Heather feels sometimes about being

blind." And Allison didn't want to admit it, especially because it seemed so petty in light of Sarah's challenges, but it was also how she felt about being the daughter of a movie star.

"It doesn't seem fair, does it?" Sarah said.

Allison shook her head and Sarah sighed. They heard the lunch bell ringing so they rowed quickly back to the dock and dashed up to the dining hall. They were late but managed to slip in quietly after Miss Campbell asked the blessing. Everyone was already eating, but Heather and Barbara had saved two places, keeping Monica at a safe distance this time.

"I signed us up for the softball tournament this afternoon," Monica announced loudly from the other end of the table. "Our cabin will play against the senior girls in Beechnut Cabin. We need *everyone* to be there." She looked directly at Heather.

"Well, I don't think you'll want me," Heather said. "I don't even know how to play. I'd surely make you lose."

"Then it's high time you learned," Monica said. "Besides, we need everyone so we can make a full team."

When lunch was over, they met out on the softball diamond. Allison and Barbara assured Heather not to worry. Monica couldn't very well force her to play against her will.

"You can be our cheering section, Heather." Barbara guided Heather to a bench behind the backstop. They gathered mitts and balls from the sports shed and warmed up in the field.

"Hey, Heather!" Monica yelled. "Come on, we need you!"

"Sorry, Monica. I'm just not up to it. Thanks anyway. I'll cheer you on."

From the outfield, Allison observed Monica walking closer to Heather, tossing a softball up and down in her hand over and over. Sensing trouble, Allison jogged across the field.

"Here, Heather, hold this." Monica threw the ball straight toward her. Heather instinctively lifted her hands, but the ball hit her smack in the face, knocking her sunglasses to the dirt. Blood instantly spurted from her nose. Allison flew to Heather's side, glaring at Monica with an intense loathing. Barbara ran up and grabbed Monica by the arm.

"What do you think you're doing?" she screamed.

"Let me go—it was an accident. I thought she'd catch it."

"My foot, you did!" Barbara yelled in Monica's face. Just then John Stewart, who was coming back from a counselors' meeting, dashed over and pulled the two girls apart.

"What's going on here?" he demanded.

"Monica just gave Heather a bloody nose!" Barbara exclaimed, pointing in Heather's direction. John looked over in alarm.

"Is that true, Monica?"

She shrugged her shoulders. "All I did is throw a ball to her. It's not like she's blind or anything. Or is she? Hey, look at those eyes. I do believe she is blind. Heather, why are you hiding—"

"Shut up, Monica!" Barbara shouted. "Just shut your mouth!"

"Allison, you get Heather to the infirmary," John instructed. "I'll deal with Monica."

Allison held her kerchief on Heather's nose to stop the bleeding as she guided her back to the main lodge. Miss Campbell was in the infirmary and sent for an ice pack to keep the swelling down.

"How did this happen, Heather?" she asked.

"She got hit with a softball," Allison explained, not ready to incriminate Miss Campbell's own niece.

"These things happen," Miss Campbell said kindly. "I don't think it's broken, and it doesn't seem to be swelling badly."

John walked in with Monica in tow and Barbara not far behind. His face was a mix of emotions.

"Miss Campbell," John said, obviously trying to keep calm. "Monica is responsible for this."

"What?" Miss Campbell gaped at her niece. "I thought it was an accident—"

"No, it seems that Heather is blind." He looked at Heather. She lay on the infirmary bed in a blood-splattered shirt with an ice pack covering her face. Miss Campbell stared at Heather in amazement.

"The girls have been trying to keep it secret," John continued. "But Monica found out and threw the softball at Heather in hopes of exposing it." Now Monica's head drooped.

"Well, I never!" Miss Campbell exclaimed. "How extraordinary! Heather, you certainly had me fooled. But why didn't you tell us?"

Heather sat up and removed the ice pack. Silent tears streamed down her cheeks. "Are you going to send me home?"

Miss Campbell put her arm around Heather. "Of course not, dear. Why in the world would we do that? My goodness, I'm very impressed that you would be so brave to come to camp and even keep your handicap a secret." She hugged Heather, and Allison could've hugged Miss Campbell.

Miss Campbell turned to Monica. "As for you, young lady, we've got plenty of jobs to keep you out of trouble. The bathrooms need a thorough scrubbing, then you can report to Cookie for KP, and I expect a full apology to Heather—later. Now march, missy!" Monica slinked out and Miss Campbell said quietly, "Monica hasn't heard the last of this—don't you worry." She marched out of the room.

"Are you okay, Heather?" Barbara asked. Heather nodded.

"Heather," John began, "why didn't you tell us? You could've told me—"

"It's hard to explain, John. It was partly fear of being sent back, but sometimes people treat me funny when they know I'm blind. For once, I wanted to be just like one of the gang."

"You are one of the gang, Heather," he said. "Being blind doesn't change anything. We all like you because you're Heather. Right, girls?"

Everyone agreed heartily. Hugs were shared and a few more tears spilled, and Allison felt as if a heavy load had been lifted. She watched John give Heather's hand a squeeze before he left.

"Hey, what do you say we all go for a swim to cool off. You want to come, Heather?" Barbara suggested.

"Sure," Heather replied with a smile.

After a rowdy swim, Allison stretched out in the sand and squinted up into the bright blue sky. It felt good to be alive. She wondered for the umpteenth time what was happening at Tamaqua Point. Just knowing they were waiting for her back in Oregon filled her with a warm feeling.

"Allison," Sarah said. "I think I'm going to write my mother a letter and tell her how it makes me feel for her to act as if Auschwitz never happened."

"Sarah, that's a great idea. Then at least she'll know, and you can get it off your chest."

Allison thought of her own mother. What was Marsha thinking about her father's attempt to gain custody? She couldn't understand why Marsha should even care, since she'd never had time for her before. Maybe Marsha would be glad if Allison lived in Oregon with her dad.

"You know, Sarah," Allison said, "maybe I should do the same thing. My mother and father are divorced, and Dad wants to have custody of me. I should write Marsha—that's my mom—and tell her what I want."

"You mean you'd rather be with your dad than your mom?" Sarah looked surprised.

"Oh sure, I've never really been with my mom much. I hardly even know her. She's always off shooting a movie some-where—" Allison realized her error. She looked at Sarah to see if she caught it, and Sarah stared in puzzlement.

Sarah looked at her suspiciously. "Your mother's name is Marsha and she makes movies? Is your mother Marsha Madison?"

Allison nodded sheepishly. "Please don't tell, Sarah. I don't want anyone to know. It's kind of like what Heather said—people won't treat you the same."

"I understand. It's like the Jewish thing for me. Wow, isn't it funny how we've all been hiding our different secrets? It's kind of neat because now I don't feel so alone."

Allison smiled. "Yep, I know just what you mean."

 Seven

THE DAYS SLOWLY BECAME WEEKS, and life at camp settled into a pleasant routine. Even Monica grew more tolerable. Camp friendships blossomed and matured to the point Allison realized saying good-bye would be tough. But her greatest concern was where she would go next. Would her home be in Oregon living with her father or on the East Coast, shuttled back and forth between boarding school, Cape Cod, and the occasional visit to Marsha's New York penthouse?

Allison always looked forward to mail, but so far the news from Oregon, though delightful to read, wasn't very encouraging when it came to the custody problem. At least her father was telling it to her straight, and it seemed he was doing all he could. Marsha, or rather Marsha's lawyers, were determined to make life difficult. But in each letter he wrote, her father assured her that everything would turn out okay in the end. She hoped he was right.

During the last week of camp, Allison decided she'd just go home with her father when he came to pick them up by train. She figured it couldn't hurt since she'd heard nothing from Marsha. Even if Marsha had to go out to Oregon to get her, at least she would have some time with the people she loved. And if Marsha came out, maybe she'd see how much Allison needed to be there. Maybe it would help Marsha to change her mind. She had never seemed to care where Allison had lived before.

"Two more days until camp ends," Heather announced at lunch.

"Doesn't seem possible," Allison said, biting into her sandwich. "But I'm so glad. I can't wait to see Dad and—"

"Grace and the boys," Heather said, finishing Allison's sentence.

"I'm going to miss you all so much," Sarah said sadly.

"Me too," Barbara chimed in. "We'll have to keep in touch. Maybe we can even plan a reunion or go and visit one another!"

"That would be swell!" Allison exclaimed. "You can come see us in Oregon. We have this really big house by the ocean." And the four girls agreed that they'd always be friends.

Allison was still basking in the warmth of her camp friendships later when she noticed a large dark blue cab parked in front of the lodge. It looked just like the car they'd ridden to camp in with Lola. Probably for some camper who was getting picked up early. Beside the car stood a fashionably dressed woman. But she looked out of place here, like a flashy flamingo on the prairie. Her bright coral dress, white hat, and gloves seemed to glare in the bright afternoon sun. Then Allison did a double take while her heart lurched in fear. It was Marsha!

Allison's first response was to run and hide, but what good would that do? They'd only find her, and she didn't want to be dragged out kicking and screaming. Slowly, as if approaching the firing squad, she walked toward the car.

"Allison," someone called from behind. "Want to take a swim?" Allison looked back to see Sarah running up the grassy slope toward her. "What's wrong, Allison? You look like you've seen a ghost."

"It's Marsha—she's here." Allison nodded her head toward the lodge. Marsha leaned casually against the porch rail and conversed with Len, who already seemed to be under her spell.

Sarah reached for Allison's hand and gave it a reassuring squeeze. "It'll be okay, Allison."

"Well, there she is," Len proclaimed warmly. "Allison, you didn't tell us your mother was the famous Marsha Madison!" His excitement was beginning to draw a small crowd. Soon, girls of all ages were dashing off in search of paper to solicit autographs. Marsha, as usual, casually ate it up, barely pausing to greet her own daughter. But then, what else was new?

"Okay, kids," Len said. "Clear the way, now. Marsha came to pick up Allison."

Allison clenched her teeth. Of course! What had she expected—that Marsha had popped in to say hello?

"Yes, dear," Marsha said. "Go gather your things. Or maybe we could have them sent later. Dear me, you do look frightful. I hope you have something decent to wear. We've a train to catch as soon as we get back to town. I hope we're not late. Goodness, this place is out in the middle of nowhere. Now hurry, Allison. Only bring what you absolutely need. I'm sure this dear gentleman will see that the rest is sent." Len nodded and Marsha handed him her card.

In a daze, Allison dashed back to the cabin and shoved some things into her suitcase. How could this be happening? What did it mean? Had her father given up?

Allison quickly cleaned up and pulled on the wrinkled green linen suit. She wondered if Marsha would recognize it, then wondered why she should even care. Her whole world was crashing down upon her, and there didn't seem to be anything she could do about it. Wasn't there any way out of this? Could she run away again? Would any resistance on her part ruin her chances of returning to Oregon?

Allison's friends were gathered by the car. Hurried hugs and good-byes were dispensed with promises to write. Last of all, Allison hugged Heather with angry tears in her eyes. This was not how it was supposed to be. She was supposed to ride the train back home with Heather and Dad.

"Allison, it will be all right," Heather whispered with conviction. "I just know it will. Please don't worry. Remember how things went with Lola? Just try to be nice to Marsha. It might help while your father is working to get you back."

Allison sniffed. "But what if—"

"No, Allison. It will work out."

"Come on, Allison," Marsha urged as she climbed into the taxi. "We have a train to catch."

Allison wanted to scream and cry and carry on like a four-year-old. Instead, she clenched her teeth in anger as she spoke. "I'm sorry, I have to go now. I'll write as soon as possible, Heather. Please tell Dad I'm sorry."

Constance looked straight into Allison's eyes. "Remember, God has answers to even our toughest questions."

Allison swallowed the lump in her throat and nodded. She believed Constance, but she wasn't sure she was ready to ask those kinds of questions.

She climbed into the taxi and waved from the backseat to all of her dear friends. Their faces were blurred by her tears. And as the driver pulled away, the camp was further obscured in a cloud of dust.

"Well, Allison," Marsha began. "Aren't you at all pleased to see your mother?"

Allison watched the curious driver eye them from the rearview mirror, obviously keenly interested in their conversation. Movie stars were probably not his ordinary fare. She wondered if he could even manage to keep his car on the road.

Allison wiped the tears from her face with the back of her hand. She was not ready to talk. She didn't know if she ever would be. She turned her face away and stared out the window. She thought about Dad and the letter and the embezzlement charges. She wanted to lash out at Marsha, but she was worried about harming her father's case. He had purposely not revealed too much to Lola and had warned Allison to do likewise. Besides, Allison wasn't eager to admit to Marsha that she had gone through her personal things in order to discover the letter.

"So you're going to give me the silent treatment, Allison? After I came all this way to see you. And I am not even angry at you for running away."

Allison turned and looked at Marsha curiously.

Marsha nodded and then waved her hands as if she were a queen pardoning a peasant from the gallows. "Yes, you are completely absolved, Allison. Not another word of it. Now, aren't you even going to ask me about my latest movie?"

Allison sighed. "How was Istanbul, Marsha?" Her voice was stiff and cold, without an ounce of real interest. Marsha seemed not to notice, or else she was just acting again.

"Absolutely horrible, darling. So smelly and hot. The people there live like animals. I am so thankful to be back to civilization." She looked out the window and frowned skeptically. "Well, I guess you could call it that."

Allison folded her arms across her chest and stared out her window. The trees whizzed by in a mass of green without any distinction from one to the next. It reminded her a little of Oregon, but thinking of Oregon right now was little comfort.

"But Stanley was such a dear," Marsha continued, oblivious to Allison's indifference. "He tried to make me comfortable whenever he could. He saw to my every whim and babied me through the entire shoot. I don't know what I would've done without him." Marsha snapped open her alligator purse, removed a shiny gold compact, and powdered her straight little nose. "It's terribly humid today. Driver, can't you open a vent or something?"

Allison fumed in silence, unable to form sensible words and

unwilling to submit to idle chatter. Marsha carried the conversation unassisted for quite a while, but eventually even she grew bored with her own babble. The driver looked disappointed, like he'd been cheated out of his entertainment.

They arrived at the station just minutes before their train was due to depart. The driver huffed after them, lugging all their baggage as they raced across the terminal. Marsha paid him generously just before they leaped aboard the train. The conductor closed the doors, the brakes squealed, and they were off.

"Thank goodness," Marsha gasped. "Can you imagine if we'd missed this train? We'd have been destined to spend the night in that awful little mining town." Allison read the name of the sign as they pulled out of the station. Dunnsville. That was Constance's hometown.

The train headed west, which seemed odd to Allison, but she didn't ask Marsha about their destination. Instead, she either kept her nose in a tattered *Saturday Evening Post* or stared blankly out the windows. They arrived in Cleveland by dinnertime.

"Come on, Allison," Marsha said. "We get out here."

As much as Allison hated to admit it, especially in light of her disappointment, it was sort of fun to travel with Marsha. They were treated like royalty wherever they went. In the hotel restaurant, no one complained when they were quickly seated, though others were left waiting and whispering about how strange it was to see Marsha Madison in town. Strains of a Glenn Miller tune sifted in from the lounge next door where a big band played. Something about the formal room with the low-lit lamps on the elegant tables made Allison feel grown-up and sophisticated, but still she remained silent, unwilling to show any pleasure in Marsha's little game.

"You know, Allison, you're not making this easy for me," Marsha said as she unfolded her napkin. "You could try to make the best of it. Just think, Allison, how many times have we been able to spend time together like this? And after all, I am your mother."

"Oh, do you want me to call you Mother now?" Allison asked in a surly tone.

Marsha fidgeted with her fork. "Well, let's stick to Marsha for the time being—you don't really mind, do you?"

Allison laughed. It was a low, cynical laugh. What difference did it make? "Mind? Of course not, Marsha. Why should I mind?"

"Allison, you look older," Marsha said, carefully changing the subject. "And I like what you've done with your hair. I was meaning to tell you last Christmas you're too old for pigtails."

Marsha's determined congeniality was getting to Allison. She'd never known Marsha to be so nice, and it made giving the cold shoulder difficult.

"Thanks, Marsha. I had it done in New York at a nice little salon on Fifth Avenue. Yes, I had a marvelous time in New York, and your penthouse is quite comfortable." Allison watched Marsha's eyebrows lift slightly.

"You stayed in my apartment while I was gone? How quaint. And your clothes?" Marsha examined Allison's suit with a knowing look.

"Yes, compliments of the Marsha Madison collection."

Marsha smiled. "It's nice to see you've got a flair for fashion, Allison. And you've grown to be—well, almost pretty."

Allison blushed. Coming from Marsha, this was quite a compliment. "Thanks. I thought it was interesting that your clothes fit me almost perfectly."

"I think you might actually be a hair taller than me, Allison. But still a bit on the skinny side." Marsha laughed, and for a second Allison thought her face looked softer. In spite of herself, Allison relaxed a little.

"Marsha, why did we come west on the train?"

"Oh, didn't I tell you, darling? We're going to Hollywood. I have to sign a contract and meet a producer and all sorts of fun things."

"And you're taking me with you?"

"Sure, I always told you I would someday. Lola is already there. She's found this fantastic house with a pool, and Stanley will come out next month. He has some unfinished business in New York."

"You mean you'll be living in Hollywood?"

"Not actually Hollywood. Beverly Hills is more like it. And we'll keep the New York apartment, but mostly we'll stay in California." Marsha took a long sip of coffee and glanced at her diamond-encrusted watch. "It's getting late and we have an early morning flight. Maybe we should call it a night."

There was so much to take in that Allison simply nodded mutely and followed Marsha to their room.

&c &c &c

The next morning, Allison stared at the small red airplane sitting on the tarmac. Were they really going up in that? She'd only seen Marsha board a large silver twin-engine plane once, and she'd never actually flown herself.

"Climb in, little lady," a man in a brown leather bomber jacket said. "My plane's name is *Ramblin' Rosie* and I'm Willy." He patted the side of the plane, and Allison climbed hesitantly into the tiny backseat. Marsha sat in front beside Willy and didn't seem a bit concerned about the size of the plane. Allison closed her eyes and held her breath as they took off. The feeling of leaving the ground proved exhilarating, and when she finally opened her eyes, she looked down in wonder.

"So what do you think of *Rosie*, little lady?" Willy called over the roar of the engine.

"She's wonderful," Allison answered. "It's amazing how everything looks so tiny. Like toy houses and barns." She watched the miniature world unfold beneath them.

"Can you reach that basket behind you?" Willy asked. Allison looked back to see a wicker picnic basket and pulled it out.

"Why don't you play the stewardess," he suggested. Allison divvied out some cookies and poured coffee.

"Sorry it's not much," Willy apologized. "Beulah was sick, and she usually packs something a tad more interesting, but her husband's running the airstrip cafe today."

They landed in Chicago just before noon. Allison thanked Willy for the flight and assured him she'd always remember her first time in a plane. They waited in the large airline terminal for their next flight.

"So you like flying?" Marsha asked as she lit a cigarette. Marsha didn't smoke very often because she said it turned her teeth yellow. Allison hated when she did; it always made her eyes burn.

"Yeah, flying's pretty neat," Allison answered. "And Willy was nice." Marsha nodded and blew out a long, slow puff.

It wasn't long until their next flight was ready to leave. Together they boarded a large plane like the one Allison had expected earlier. They sat in first class at the front of the plane. Other passengers spoke in low tones, recognizing and admiring Marsha. Surprisingly, Allison experienced an unwelcome swell of pride.

Once she was settled in her comfortable seat, Allison studied her mother. Marsha was wearing a soft pink embossed silk suit adorned with pearls. Her hair was styled perfectly beneath her wide-brimmed matching hat, and, for once, her lipstick wasn't such a harsh tone of red. Allison wondered if Marsha was changing her image. This was the most conservative ensemble she'd ever seen her wear.

"Hi, I'm Betty," a pretty blond stewardess announced. "Lunch will be ready in a few minutes. Can I bring you a drink, Miss Madison?"

When Marsha had placed her order, Allison asked for orange juice. Betty handed her a recent issue of *Vogue* with a photo of Lauren Bacall on the front.

"Dear me, I'm famished," Marsha exclaimed. She carefully removed her hat and gloves and leaned back. "Famished and tired. All this traveling will take its toll on me, I'm afraid." She slipped the gold compact out of her white kid purse and studied her reflection. "I haven't slept well since I left New York, and it's starting to show. It's a good thing I had Lola make us an appointment at Viola's."

"Us?" Allison questioned. "What's Viola's?"

"Just the most fantastic salon in Beverly Hills."

Allison stared openly at Marsha. She couldn't believe Marsha had made an appointment for the two of them together. Before she could comment, the stewardess returned with their meal and Marsha began eating.

After lunch, Marsha stared blankly out the window until she stretched back and fell asleep. Allison watched her mother dozing next to her and experienced the closest thing to affection she'd ever felt. She remembered Constance sharing about how she'd forgiven her father. Allison wondered if she could ever do the same with Marsha. She peered out the window at the tops of the white clouds. They reminded her of the fluffy meringue Muriel heaped upon her lemon pies back in Oregon. Right now, Tamaqua Point seemed like a lifetime away.

Eight

THE SUN HUNG BIG AND RED on the horizon as they landed at the Los Angeles airport. Harsh lights lined the runway in stark contrast to the soft rose-colored sky. Marsha adjusted her hat and pulled on her gloves, and Allison did likewise, then instantly wished she hadn't. She'd only been with Marsha one day and already she was copying her mannerisms. In the air terminal, they soon spotted Lola waving both arms, and they pressed through the crowd toward her.

"You're here at last!" Lola exclaimed, taking Marsha's bag. "And how was Istanbul?"

"Don't ask," Marsha moaned. "Can we get someone to deliver the rest of our luggage?"

"It's all arranged. Just come with me." They followed Lola out to the waiting limousine and climbed in. Allison watched in fascination as the Southern California sights passed by.

Before long they were in Beverly Hills. The colors seemed brighter than normal, and the tall palm trees and other exotic-looking foliage was like entering another country. The limousine pulled into a driveway lined with yet more tall palms. The driveway circled in front of a large, pinkish stucco house that was illuminated by spotlights and loomed before them like a strange tropical palace from a movie set.

"Well, Lola," Marsha commented. "It definitely has that California look I wanted. Actually, it seems quite nice."

They stepped into the expansive entrance, and Allison gaped at the lavish decor. A carved stone lion sat in the center of a fountain that bubbled beneath a curly wrought-iron stair-case. All around the fountain grew lush green plants that flour-ished like a miniature Garden of Eden.

"Italian marble," Lola explained, tapping her toe on the shiny floor. "The fountain came from a French villa, and the chandeliers are from Madrid." She led them upstairs and showed Marsha her room, a spacious suite with a large sunken tub carved out of another giant slab of white marble. French doors opened onto a wrought-iron terrace that was lined with blooming flower pots, splashing out even more vibrant color.

"Very nice," said Marsha, laying her handbag on the bed. "And I'm dying to try out that tub."

"I'll call Isobella, the upstairs maid, to draw your bath," Lola said, closing the ornately carved door behind her. Allison fol-lowed Lola down the hall. "Your bedroom is on the right at the end of this hallway. Do you want me to show you?"

"No, Lola, I can find it, thanks."

"Say, how did it go with Heather at camp?" Lola asked in a conspiratory tone.

"Just fine. Heather had a great time."

Allison opened the door at the end of the hall expecting to find a small, impersonal room, something akin to the one in Marsha's New York penthouse. Instead, she discovered a large, comfortable room with an adjoining bath. The luxury seemed even more foreign after her previous weeks of bunking in a rus-tic log cabin.

Her watch was still set on camp time, and she figured they would just be ending the campfire by now. It would be the last campfire of the summer. Tomorrow her father would be there. *What will he do when he finds out I'm gone?* she wondered. The thought of his disappointed face placed a large lump in her throat, and she socked a bed pillow in anger.

"Here's your bag, miss," an older man outside her open door said. "I'm Adam, the butler, miss. Where can I put it for you?"

"Right there is fine," said Allison, wiping an angry tear with the back of her hand.

"Everything okay, miss?" he asked kindly.

She forced a smile. "Just missing someone."

"Oh, I know how that goes, miss."

"My name's Allison."

He smiled. "Fine, Miss Allison. If I can be of any help, just call." He turned crisply and walked away.

Allison started unpacking her suitcase. Had she remembered to pack her letters? She dug until she found them buried on the bottom, tied with a satin ribbon. She slowly reread each one and felt comforted by the knowledge that her father was still working to get her back.

⁖ ⁖ ⁖

The next morning, Isobella brought a tray into Allison's room. This was something new. Allison had never been served breakfast in bed before, not even at Tamaqua Point—although Muriel had tried once.

"Good morning, Allison. I'm Isobella," the maid announced curtly. She clanked the tray down noisily on the bedside stand and turned.

"Thank you," Allison said as Isobella disappeared. "And it's so very nice to meet you," she called to the back of the door.

Allison looked up at the clock and saw it was already after nine. She didn't normally sleep this late, but last night she'd stayed up long past midnight writing letters to everyone in Oregon. Now a neat stack of envelopes lay on the white vanity table. She stretched and looked about the room. The walls were a deep salmon color, and the furniture was all white-enameled

French Provincial. The bedspread was covered in big peach-colored cabbage roses and leafy vines. This bedroom could have sprung from a page of the latest decorator's magazine, but it couldn't hold a candle to her room back in Grandpa's house. Like her room in Oregon, this one also overlooked a garden. Only this garden looked more like a tropical paradise, full of unusual plants with spiky leaves and bright, succulent flowers. Allison finished her breakfast, pulled on some shorts and a blouse, and decided to explore her new home.

Marsha's door was closed, and Allison tiptoed past and down the stairs. She found several rooms that all looked much the same. What interested her most was the game room at the end of the house, complete with a large green billiards table and big glass doors that opened out to a sumptuous swimming pool wrapped in a large tiled deck. She opened the doors and walked out to get a better look at the pool. It was shaped like a giant four-leaf clover and bordered with ornately painted tiles. Wooden outdoor furniture with fresh blue-and-white-striped cushions lazed around the deck. It looked like a perfect place for fun times of swimming and relaxing in the sun. And it made Allison mad to think that it appealed to her. She felt like she was selling out to the enemy.

"So, Allison, what do you think?" Lola asked from behind her. Allison turned in surprise. There stood Lola with an icy drink and cigarette, clad in bright yellow clam diggers and a cropped white top. Allison had never seen her in anything but business clothes, and this new side of Lola was slightly amusing. Lola sat down on a deck chair and took a long drag from her cigarette.

"It's very nice," Allison said.

"Nice, nice . . . You sound just like your mother! It's more than nice, it's fantastic! I did a terrific job, and if no one else will admit it, I'll just have to compliment myself." Lola reached over her own shoulder and patted herself on the back.

Allison laughed. "Okay, Lola, it's swell! It's beautiful! Are you content now?"

Lola smiled smugly and adjusted her rhinestone-rimmed dark glasses. "We'll be going to town at eleven. I've made appointments at Viola's and then we'll go shopping."

"Lola," Allison asked quietly. "Can you tell me why Marsha is being so nice to me?"

Lola shrugged and blew out a puff of blue smoke. "Don't be concerned, Allison. Just enjoy."

Allison stared at the glistening pool and pondered Lola's words. Well, why not? There was nothing she could do about her circumstances, so why fight it? "Okay, Lola. I think I'll take a quick dip before I get ready to go."

Lola nodded and sipped her drink. "Smart girl."

After a delicious swim, Allison lounged on a deck chair and towel dried her hair in the morning sun. Soon Marsha came out wrapped in a satiny white robe. She stretched and yawned and lazily dipped a well-manicured toe into the pool.

"We'll be leaving in half an hour, Allison. We'll go straight to Viola's, so don't worry about how you look, but bring along something nice to wear afterward. That peach suit looked all right, but you better have Isobella iron it a bit."

The driver dropped them off at the back of Viola's, and Allison noticed a woman who looked a lot like Bette Davis furtively glance over her shoulder as she emerged from her white limousine. The clandestine back entrance reminded Allison of a secret club. Inside, they were greeted by a pretty, dark-haired woman dressed in a crisp lavender uniform.

"Marsha Madison!" she gushed, taking her by the hand. "We haven't seen you in ages. Viola will take care of you personally.

And who have we here?" She looked at Allison.

"This is my sister, Allison. She'll have the treatment, too."

Allison wondered what the treatment might be. Perhaps some sort of medieval torture? She snickered as she submissively followed another lavender lady up the purple-carpeted staircase. Her name tag identified her as Tessa, and she handed Allison a large white towel.

"First, you'll enjoy a nice, soothing sauna," Tessa said. "Only twenty minutes, though—then meet me out here."

In less than ten minutes, Allison could stand the heat no longer and burst out of the claustrophobic room, gasping for air. A sweaty gray-haired woman rolled her eyes at Allison and flipped the page of her magazine.

"Allison, that was awfully quick," Tessa said, glancing at her watch.

"Sorry, it's all I could take."

Tessa smiled. "No matter, come on in here and Greta will give you a rubdown."

Greta, a large blond woman, pummeled and pounded Allison's body like a piece of raw meat. She gently rubbed in a cool ointment that smelled like fresh mint.

"*Das gut*, now you feel gut all day," Greta announced with satisfaction. Surprisingly, when Allison stood up she did feel good, and her muscles were loose and relaxed.

"Thanks, Greta," Allison said as she tied her purple robe self-consciously around her. Tessa magically appeared once more and led Allison to a mirrored room filled with bright purple chairs. Beauticians and manicurists flitted around the seated patrons like bees to flowers.

Allison sat in a chair and sighed. All this attention was kind of nice. She hated to admit it, but this was something she could get used to. And she was pretty sure that she had spied Elizabeth Taylor's famous violet eyes behind a facial masque. Not that Allison was one to have her head turned by movie stars. She thought they were all superficial and vain, but still it was amusing to see them in person. She would never dream of asking one for an autograph or making a big to-do, but it might be fun to tell Heather and Grace about it later—that is, if there would be a later.

Tessa introduced Allison to a hairdresser who shampooed and conditioned her hair, then trimmed it up a bit. Meanwhile, a manicurist was painting her nails a bright coral. Allison had never worn nail polish, but she'd decided to take Lola's advice and just enjoy. The hairdresser rolled her damp hair in tight metal curlers, then sent her over to the cosmetologist.

"Hi, I'm Andrea," a young woman with a painted-on face greeted her. "I'll do your makeup."

Allison stared at Andrea's face in horror. "Uh . . . okay, but I don't really wear makeup, so can you go easy . . . please?"

Andrea nodded, then quickly slapped a mud facial mask on her and vanished.

Allison leaned back in the chair and tried to relax, but the curlers were starting to make her head hurt and her face felt like it was encased in quick-drying cement. Just when she feared she couldn't take it anymore, Andrea appeared with a tall glass of cola and a straw.

"Sip carefully so you don't crack your face," Andrea warned. Allison almost laughed when she considered how she might actually look with a cracked face. Andrea leaned over close to Allison and whispered, "Don't look now, but that's Bette Davis over there. I think she still looks pretty good for her age. She must be around forty."

Finally the mask and curlers were removed, and Andrea applied step after tedious step of cosmetics. Allison felt certain she'd end up looking exactly like a clown when she was done. Her one consolation was that, aside from Marsha and Lola, no one in California knew her. Andrea spun the chair around, and Allison looked timidly into the mirror. It wasn't quite as bad as she'd expected, and the colors were softer, but it felt like a mask and she longed to scrape it off. Just then Marsha strolled up wearing a purple robe like Allison's.

"Not bad, Allison. Makes you look older." Then Marsha's brow furrowed slightly as if maybe that wasn't a good thing. "Let's get dressed and have some lunch. Lola's made reservations at Verve's."

They dined at the popular Beverly Hills club, and Allison recognized several famous faces. She spotted Mickey Rooney and was amazed at how short he really was. And there was the elegant Lauren Bacall in a tan dress. Allison did admire Miss Bacall's hair; she wished she could get hers to stay that smooth and silky.

People streamed past their table chatting with Marsha without really saying anything, their only concern to make a good show. Most of the faces were not familiar to Allison. They were probably lesser-known actors or worked behind the cameras. Allison sat quietly in her chair like a spectator watching a peculiar parade, where everyone struts around without any genuine interest in anyone else.

The highlight of lunch was when Katharine Hepburn walked in. Now here was an actress that Allison suspected might have more depth to her. Maybe it was the roles Katharine played, or maybe just the way she carried herself with such sweet dignity, but Allison had to admit that Katharine Hepburn might be different—at least different from Marsha Madison.

After lunch they shopped along Rodeo Drive. Allison wondered why Marsha didn't just go to a department store instead of all these little expensive shops. They perused Mario's and Vivianno's and on and on until Allison lost track of the names. In one shop where almost everything seemed to be some shade of blue, Allison spotted Doris Day selecting a pale blue evening dress.

Allison flopped down in a chair that had just been vacated by a bald, portly gentleman who must've been wearing half a dozen big diamond rings. He'd been waiting for a young, pretty woman who was apparently his wife but could have passed for his daughter. Allison leaned back and tried to remember all the things they had already purchased—didn't they have enough already? Marsha probably wanted to make sure that Allison's appearance didn't embarrass her in front of all her movie friends.

"What do you think, Allison?" Marsha asked, spinning around in a sapphire blue sequined evening gown.

Allison stared in amazement. Marsha's eyes matched the gown perfectly, and her skin glowed creamy white against the rich jewel-tone color. Her black hair gleamed in competition with the glittering gown. "It's fantastic, Marsha," Allison answered truthfully.

"I'll take it," Marsha announced to the smiling little man.

He clasped his pudgy hands together and gushed, "Yes, yes, you'll love it! An original. Very good, Miss Madison."

"We'll have a big party when Stanley gets here, Allison. And I'll wear this gown, and I'll invite everybody who's anybody in Beverly Hills."

As they drove to Marsha's new home, Allison experienced a tidal wave of guilt. What was she doing here, sitting in the back of a plush limo, decked to the nines? She belonged in Oregon with her father and her real friends. All day she had been telling herself that she had no use for this glitzy, shallow movie-star lifestyle. But if that was really the truth, why was she enjoying it so much?

Nine

DAY AFTER DAY, Allison checked the mail pile on the entry table. After two weeks with absolutely no responses from anyone in Oregon, she became concerned and hurt. Were they so absorbed with life that they'd completely forgotten her? Were they annoyed with her for going with Marsha? She had faithfully written letters to Dad, Andrew, Grace, and Heather, explaining to them where she was. She'd even written to George and Muriel and sent a postcard to Winston. And still nothing.

"Ready to go to the country club?" Marsha asked brightly. So far almost every day had been packed with events: luncheons, picnics, teas, tennis parties, and whatever else came up. Marsha devoured the attention, claiming she'd been socially starved in Istanbul. Besides, she had to maintain her very influential connections to her career.

"Marsha, I think I'll beg out today," Allison said. "If you don't mind, I'll just hang around the house." Marsha looked at her with suspicion, then agreed.

Marsha had continued to be congenial and pleasant—at least for Marsha. She'd only lost her temper a couple of times, but not anything serious. And although self-absorbed, Marsha actually showed a fragment of interest in Allison. Still, she never allowed Allison to discuss her father or their upcoming custody squabble. But Allison bided her time and hoped that someday she would penetrate the invisible wall that Marsha seemed to have erected around herself. The scary thing was that Allison had begun to care for Marsha. Though she hated to admit it, she hoped perhaps Marsha cared about her as well.

Allison took her stationery box out by the pool and wrote letters describing how unhappy she was with the way that no one had written to her. After almost an hour, she sealed and addressed the last envelope. It was to Andrew. She stretched back in her lounge chair and wondered what he might be doing right now. She imagined him out in the rowboat fishing with her father. But instead of comforting her like it used to, the image only frustrated her. She should be out in the rowboat with them! And as much as she cared for Andrew, in her mind's eye she tossed him overboard and took his place, then snickered out loud at her own silliness.

"Private joke?" Lola asked as she strolled out onto the deck. Allison glanced over her shoulder and shook her head, resenting Lola's intrusion into her daydream.

"Been writing letters?" Lola nodded to the obvious pile of stationery. Lola pulled out a silver case and retrieved a cigarette.

"I wonder why I bother," Allison complained. "No one seems to care. I haven't heard a word from anyone. I can't understand it, Lola. I thought at least Dad would write."

Lola looked out across the pool without answering, then put her cigarette back in the case and shrugged her shoulders. "I don't know, Allison. But I wouldn't worry about it too much." She stood up and went back into the house.

Allison had thought it strange at first that Lola lived in Marsha's house, but then Lola had explained that it made it handy for handling Marsha's personal and professional business, plus Marsha didn't have to pay Lola as much salary. Allison figured that Lola was enjoying this small slice of Beverly Hills pie, something she would surely not have been able to afford on her secretary's budget.

"Care for some iced tea, Miss Allison?" Adam asked.

She looked up at the butler dressed as usual in his neat black uniform and looking so out of place by the pool. She nodded and thanked him as he handed her a tall, icy glass with a lemon slice wedged on the rim. But he didn't turn to leave.

"Would you like me to see that those letters get mailed?" Adam offered, eyeing the neat stack of envelopes.

"Sure, Adam. Thanks."

He remained on the deck, casting a cool shadow upon her and fiddling with the silver tray in his hands. "You have friends in Oregon, do you, Miss Allison?"

"Yes," she answered eagerly. "How did you know?"

"Well, I—uh," he stared at the letters and she followed his gaze to the envelopes lying face down, giving no clue as to their destination. She studied him intensely. How did he know they were bound for Oregon?

"Adam?" she questioned, a thought suddenly occurring to her. "Who brings in the mail every day?"

"I do, miss." He looked over to the garden and shifted his feet. Beads of sweat appeared on his brow as the sun beat down with no mercy on his dark wool suit.

"And then you put the mail on the stand in the entryway—right?"

"Well, no, not exactly. . ."

"Not exactly? What do you mean—where do you put the mail?"

"I've been instructed by Miss Madison to give all mail to Miss Stevens so she can sort it."

Allison scratched her head. It didn't take a genius to figure this one out. She stood up and looked him in the eye. "Adam, have you ever seen any mail addressed to me from Oregon?"

"I may be putting my job on the line here, Miss Allison, but I think the truth is more important. Yes, there's been a lot of mail from Oregon. I suppose you haven't seen any of it."

Allison sighed and slumped into the lounge chair. Adam pulled up another chair and sat beside her. "Do you want to tell me about it, Allison?"

She looked into his flushed face and knew he was sweltering in the noonday sun. "Sure, but let's find some shade first."

He glanced over his shoulder, and Allison remembered Lola was inside and might question a prolonged conversation with the butler.

"Meet me in the kitchen in twenty minutes," Adam said.

Allison put her things upstairs, then slipped back down to the kitchen. She peeked in Lola's opened office door, but Lola was engrossed in a thick book. Sometimes Allison wondered what Lola did all day as Marsha's secretary.

Allison went into the kitchen and was greeted by a large black woman in a calico apron. "Well, you must be Allison," the woman said as she extended a warm handshake and genuine smile. "I'm Gertie, the cook. Adam told me you was coming." She spoke in a confidential tone. "Adam and me has been thinking—something's not straight around here. And we's afraid you're the one caught right smack in the middle. It's just not fair that a girl can't have her own letters. In fact, I think there's a law against monkeying with other people's mail."

Adam walked in and straddled a chrome kitchen chair. "Have a seat, Miss Allison," he began, "and tell us what all this secrecy is about. Why does Miss Stevens confiscate your mail?"

Gertie set a big plate of sugar cookies on the table and placed a glass of milk in front of Allison. "You go right ahead, honey, you can trust me and Adam."

Allison looked into Gertie's sincere brown eyes and believed her. She told them everything she could think of. Lately she'd understood how Sarah must've felt when her mother tried to keep her from bringing up the past. At last Allison finished and she took a long swig of milk.

"Ooowee, child, that's one heavy load for you to bear!" Gertie exclaimed. "I sure hope that daddy of yours can pull this off. Say, ain't it mail time now, Adam? Maybe Miss Allison can walk down to the box with you . . ."

Adam grinned. "I wouldn't mind the company."

There in the shiny brass box lay a small stack of letters. Adam sorted them slowly so Allison could see.

"There's one," she cried and snatched it. "And another!" They were from her father and Andrew. As they walked up the long driveway, she tucked them in her shirt.

"You know, Allison, I don't see why I couldn't separate your mail for you. I'll make sure it gets to you from now on."

"Thanks, Adam. Thanks for everything." She dashed up to her room and closed the door, eager to read her letters in private and as many times as she liked. She read the one from her father first.

Dear Allison,

I get the impression by your last letter that you haven't received any mail. This is very odd, since between all of us here in Tamaqua Point we think we've written over twenty letters. The only thing I can imagine is someone is taking them, and I don't mean to accuse Marsha, but I am suspicious. If you get this letter, I'll be surprised. At least we've heard a lot from you, and in spite of the predicament, you seem to be having a pretty good time. That's a relief to everyone.

I have good news. I've actually sold several paintings at the gallery! It's very exciting, especially since some of the buyers are from different areas of the country. One man from the East Coast was so enthusiastic about my work, he offered to try to arrange a showing in New York. That brings me to something else. We now have a court date. September 17 in New York City, since that's where the custody papers are filed. That's only three weeks away, Allison. We're all curious if you will start school in Los Angeles. Heather and Andrew are desperately hoping you will get to go to Port View High with them. In fact, we've taken the liberty to pre-register you there.

We caught about a dozen crabs yesterday and cooked them on the beach. It would've been perfect if only you'd been here. I won't go on because it's my fear you'll never read these words. But Grace said she's going to pray hard that this gets through. Leave it to Grace.

All my love,
Dad

Allison almost danced around the room. Less than three weeks now! And she was already registered for school in Port View. She was so excited her fingers trembled as she tried to open Andrew's letter. It was filled with more news and his concerns of being a lighthouse keeper. As usual, he ended by saying how much he missed her. She clutched the letter to her chest and mentally erased the vision she'd had of throwing him overboard.

"Allison," Marsha called, knocking on her door.

Allison frantically stuffed the letters under her pillow. "Yes, come in," Allison said, hoping her voice sounded normal.

"We've been invited to the Healeys' for dinner at eight—"

"I don't think I want—"

"No, Allison, you must come! They've invited several young people and specifically want you there. I won't listen to another word. You'll have a fantastic time. Wear that cream satin. It'll be perfect." Marsha turned and shut the door before Allison could protest.

Allison threw herself across the bed. Even though Marsha pretended to care, she was still the same conniving, cold-hearted person she'd always been. Maybe she should confront Lola and demand her mail. Then she remembered Grace's advice to cooperate and Constance's words on forgiveness. Well, she'd tried to cooperate, but where had that gotten her? And for the moment, forgiveness was out of the question. Suddenly, a new plan began to form in Allison's mind.

Tonight she'd play Marsha's game in Marsha's style and see how Marsha liked it. She'd had a couple of weeks to observe Marsha up close and in action. She knew her little tricks like the back of her hand. And as much as Allison hated to admit, there was a bit of an actress in her, too.

Allison jumped up to search through her closet. She pulled out the cream satin dress with its wide, circular skirt, but she tossed it to the floor. Instead, she chose a sophisticated orange dress and held it up to the mirror. It was a sleeveless gown with a low back and much too old for Allison. Marsha had bought it for herself, then decided she didn't like the color and gave it to Allison. She had immediately stuck the slinky-looking gown in her closet, never dreaming she'd wear such a thing. But tonight it looked like just the ticket. She slipped on the filmy garment and pinned her hair up with a set of rhinestone combs. She laughed at her image in the floor-length mirror and liberally applied some makeup that Marsha had given her.

"My, my, you look rather . . . grown up," Marsha said with a lifted brow when Allison sauntered down the stairs. Allison was already in character. And what a character it would be. Allison smirked as she climbed into the car with Marsha behind her.

The house was in the ritziest section of Beverly Hills. Allison feigned nonchalance as they entered the lavish mansion. She was determined to stick with her plan.

"Mrs. Healey, this is my sister, Allison," Marsha said, watching Allison out of the corner of her eye.

"Delighted to meet you, dear," the stout platinum-haired hostess said in a deep voice that was probably considered sophisticated in some circles.

"Yes, I should think so," Allison replied in an equally pompous tone. "Nice little dive you've got here."

The woman blinked in surprise, and Marsha smiled apologetically. Allison flitted about like a true social butterfly, acting bored, sophisticated, overdramatic, and silly. She was trying to mimic Marsha—only more so. The disturbing thing was some people actually seemed to like it. Before long, Allison had several young men catering to her every whim, and she felt just like Scarlett O'Hara with a string of beaux following her around. She knew Marsha's eyes were on her and from time to time wished she could read her mother's thoughts. Her goal was to make Marsha furious.

As usual, Marsha had her own cluster of male admirers, too. Allison wondered what Stanley thought of Marsha's flirtations. Did he just consider it part of the package that came with marrying an actress? Allison noticed that Marsha seemed more focused on a particularly attractive gentleman. He appeared only moderately interested in Marsha, and he looked to be at least ten years her junior. This gave Allison a rather sinister idea that was fueled even more when she remembered her stolen letters. She slipped right up next to Marsha.

"Hello there, Marsh darling," Allison said with a sigh. "This party is really rather dull, don't you think?" Marsha studied her doubtfully.

"Oh, excuse me," Allison said to the man. Then she attempted her most flirtatious smile, complete with a slight fluttering of eyelashes just the way she'd seen Marsha do. "I'm Marsha's kid sister, Allison." She extended her hand and he took it in his own.

"Very pleased to meet you, Allison," he said with a smile. "I had no idea Marsha had such a lovely sister. I'm Hartley Henshaw."

Allison smiled faintly. "Well, suddenly the party seems a whole lot brighter, Hartley." She glanced at Marsha and noticed a definite glare. Very satisfying.

"Allison, do you live here in Beverly Hills or are you just visiting?" Hartley asked.

"Oh, I live with Marsh. She's such a dear to let her baby sister horn in on her and hubby like this. So sweet, but then Marsh is like that. You know, Hartley, she's been almost like a mother to me." Allison laughed. "Of course, you're not quite old enough to be my mother, are you, Marsh?" Allison shook her finger under Marsha's nose in a teasing way. "Oh, but it's close, isn't it?"

Marsha looked like she might explode, but Allison didn't care. She continued to chat with Hartley, teasing Marsha without mercy. All the while she watched with satisfaction as her mother simmered and fumed.

"I think it's time to go, Allison," Marsha seethed.

"If you need to leave early I can bring Allison home later," Hartley suggested eagerly.

"I don't think so," Marsha said curtly. She grabbed Allison by the arm.

"Oh, it's really no problem," Hartley said firmly.

Suddenly, Allison realized she could easily get in over her head. Although this game brought an interesting sense of power, it was quickly losing its appeal.

"Thanks anyway, Hartley," Allison said lightly. "I better get Marsh home. She needs her beauty rest, you know."

Marsha smoldered in angry silence as they rode home. This was so unlike Marsha, who usually freely displayed her feelings for the world to see. Allison felt slightly cheated that Marsha didn't actually explode and carry on a little. But Marsha just sat there, arms folded tightly across her chest and teeth clenched. Allison began to feel just a little bit ashamed. After all, Marsha had been trying so hard lately, and Allison didn't exactly know for sure that Marsha had kept those letters. It was entirely possible Lola controlled that area.

"Allison, I am so angry I can't even trust myself to speak," Marsha said. "But I've got to know—what on earth got into you tonight?"

"I don't know, Marsha. I just thought I'd try something new. I thought maybe you'd like it if I imitated you."

"Is that how you think I act?"

"Well, not exactly. I might have exaggerated it some."

Marsha stared at Allison with wide eyes, as if she couldn't quite believe what she had just heard. Suddenly, Marsha burst into laughter. "Poor Hartley," she gasped between giggles. "You really had him going!"

Despite herself, Allison began to laugh, too. Soon they were in hysterics over poor Hartley and what he must think of the crazy Madison sisters.

Ten

ALLISON LAY IN HER BED the next morning in turmoil. The mail dilemma still bothered her, but now that she and Adam had devised their plan, she wondered if she should just forget the whole thing for the time being. Besides, maybe she and Marsha were even now, especially after how she'd behaved at the party.

Marsha and Lola had left early to meet with Marsha's agent for some contract negotiations. Allison wandered around the empty house and finally wound up in the kitchen.

"How you doing, sugar?" Gertie asked as she rolled out some dough on the shiny stainless steel counter. Allison scooted a chrome stool over to watch Gertie work. This kitchen, with all its new post-war appliances and conveniences, was such a contrast to Muriel's old-fashioned one. But being around Gertie made Allison feel cozy even if the kitchen wasn't.

"You s'pose your mama will get her contract renewed okay?"

"Oh sure, I guess so." Actually, Allison hadn't given it much thought. She just assumed Marsha, as usual, would get what she wanted.

"I dunno, honey. I been reading them movie magazines your mama throws in the trash. They be saying that brown hair ain't popular no more in Hollywood these days. They like younger women, and, well, we know your mama ain't no spring chicken—though she do look mighty good for her age." Gertie expertly flopped the thin layer of dough into a pie plate and quickly trimmed the edges.

"Hmm, I don't know, Gertie. I wonder what Marsha would do if she couldn't get a contract. . . ." Allison watched Gertie fill the crust with luscious peach slices and sugar. "That smells yummy, Gertie."

"Yes, nothin' like the smell of fresh peaches." She handed Allison a nice ripe peach. "They're come from up in Oregon."

Allison studied the fuzzy peach in her hand. Two and a half weeks seemed a lifetime away.

After lunch, she lounged around the pool and wrote more letters, letting her dad know she'd finally heard from him. She tried not to go into much detail about the confiscated mail. There would be time to tell him all that later. Allison stuck her feet in the pool, but she had no desire to swim today. If only Dad and Grace and the Amberwells were here, then it would be fun.

Allison thought about the summer coming to an end. She wondered if Marsha had made any plans for her schooling. Allison couldn't imagine going to school in Beverly Hills, though she didn't think it would really come down to that. But just the same, she was afraid to ask. What if Marsha really wanted Allison around? What if she was finally ready to be a mom?

Doors slammed inside the house, and Allison knew Marsha and Lola were back. She entered the living room just in time to hear Marsha ranting in a loud voice.

"I am totally fed up with that studio, Lola! I've a mind to drop them altogether! Just who do they think they are? That contract stinks and they know it—what an insult!"

"Settle down, Marsha," Lola said in a soothing yet authoritative voice. "You need to stop and look at this objectively. Your last movie wasn't exactly a smash hit, and this Istanbul flick is already making the studio nervous. I've been helping to negotiate this deal for weeks, and I swear it's the best offer you're going to get."

"Well, it stinks!" Marsha stomped up the stairs and slammed her bedroom door.

Lola stomped past Allison and down the hallway. "What are you staring at?" she growled.

Allison scurried up to her room and closed the door. She felt trapped—imprisoned. If only she could escape or run away . . . But what good would come of that? Instead, she pulled out her journal and read over the poems she'd written during the summer months. She remembered Amanda on the train and how much she'd enjoyed their discussions on Emily Dickinson and poetry. Amanda had encouraged Allison to keep writing, so Allison picked up her pen.

My Prison Palace

My prison is a pretty one,
With fountains, pools, and flowers.
But it's like a dungeon deep,
Or high impenetrable towers.
My captress is quite beautiful,
With maids and ladies waiting.
But her heart is made of ice,
And her voice is grating.
I must keep hope alive,
To help me through this day.
Perhaps a knight will come for me,
And carry me away.

She closed her journal and laughed—a brave knight! *Who would that be?* she thought. Dad? Or maybe Andrew? But what if they couldn't rescue her? What if she had to stay with Marsha forever? She knew some girls would die for an opportunity to live in Beverly Hills with a movie star. She remembered awful Shirley Jenson, who had flirted with Andrew and made Allison so jealous. Shirley would think this was a fantasy come true. Or even Mr. O'Conner's daughter in Portland—her dream was to be a movie star. She would love this. Life sure wasn't fair.

By the end of the week, Marsha announced they would be returning to New York to tie up some loose ends.

"But I thought Stanley was taking care of everything and then coming out here," Allison said. The idea of returning to the East Coast filled her with an even worse sense of foreboding—it would take her farther from her father.

"There's been a change in plans, and Stanley can't take care of everything," Marsha said with that familiar edge to her voice. "We leave Saturday morning—just be ready!"

Allison dashed to her room and quickly wrote a letter to her father. As she wrote, she realized he would probably have to go to New York as well for the trial. She would see him there! Then she could return with him to Oregon. With this in mind, she eagerly packed her bags and literally counted the hours until Saturday.

It was almost time for the mail to arrive, and Allison slipped downstairs to meet Adam in the kitchen. He was seated at the table sipping a cup of coffee. This was his break time, and Allison had recently made it a habit to join Adam and Gertie when possible. It was a highlight of her day.

"Morning, sugar," Gertie greeted. "I hear you and your mama is going to New York. I ain't never been on one of those airplanes, and I don't never wanna go on one! When I look at them little specks up in the sky, I can't believe there's real people up in that. Not Gertie!" She laughed and Allison smiled. She'd sure miss Gertie.

"I hope everything turns out all right," Adam said. "But I

have to admit, I'll miss you if you go back to Oregon, Allison."

"Me too, sugar," Gertie chimed in. "But you'll come visit your mama, won't you?"

"Of course! And I'll visit you two, as well. After all, you've been like family to me." Allison looked at them sadly. "But you understand how much I need to be with my dad."

"Sure we do, honey," Gertie said. "Your mama will be so busy when her next movie starts, you'll never see her no how."

"And from what you've told us, Oregon sounds like a nice place," Adam added. "A good place for a girl to grow up." He glanced at his watch.

"Mail time?" Allison asked. He nodded, and she checked down the hallway to make sure Lola wasn't watching.

There were three letters for Allison, one from her father, one from Andrew, and one from Constance. The one from her camp counselor surprised her. How in the world did Constance get her address in Beverly Hills?

"Lola's straight ahead," Adam warned in a low voice.

Allison tucked the letters under her arm and took off across the gardens toward the pool and up the back stairway to her room. Breathlessly, she collapsed on her bed and opened the letter from Constance first.

Dear Allison,

Heather wrote and gave me your address in Beverly Hills. I hope you don't mind. I've thought about you a lot since camp and felt I should write. We had some good talks, Allison, but I never knew for sure if I really told you what was in my heart. For some reason, I think we're a little bit alike. I know our lives are worlds apart, but I got the feeling you have the same problem with your mom as I had with my dad. Unforgiveness.

I want to remind you how I was unable to forgive my dad

on my own. It took God's help. I never could've done it with-
out Him. Sometimes I thought I had forgiven my dad, but I
hadn't. The only way God could help me to forgive him was
when I asked. So I guess that's what I wanted to share. You
know, God doesn't expect us to be perfect. He just wants us
to believe in Him and ask Him for help with our lives, and
He'll show us the way. I hope you're having a good time in
Beverly Hills. It sounds pretty exciting! Write me if you want.

> *Love and God bless you,*
> *Constance*

Allison folded the letter and put it aside. She'd been getting
along with Marsha pretty well lately. Forgiveness didn't seem to
be such a problem anymore. She read the other letters. Dad was
getting set to go to New York, and it sounded like Grace might
even accompany him. He said Grace wasn't about to send him
off to New York alone again—not after that last time. In Andrew's letter, he described the first day at high school. He was
already on the football team. Allison imagined watching him
from the grandstands with the other kids on a crisp fall evening.
Suddenly, life was full of promise again. It had to work out. It
just *had* to!

∾ ∾ ∾

The next morning, Allison and Marsha boarded a large plane
bound for New York. This time Allison walked on with confidence. She remembered what Gertie had said about airplanes
and laughed. But halfway through the flight, the plane began to
lurch and bounce wildly. Food trays clattered to the floor, loose
items and hand luggage slid off of shelves, and everyone was
instructed to buckle up fast. Allison looked over at Marsha. Her
belt was unbuckled and her face was pasty white.

"Marsha, are you okay?" Allison asked. She reached across her mother's lap and quickly buckled her in. Marsha didn't even react but sat frozen, eyes wide. "It's okay, Marsha," Allison said soothingly. "The stewardess said it's just turbulence."

Marsha clung to Allison's arm. "Thanks," she muttered. "I should be used to this by now, but it always gets me. I envision the plane plummeting down like a rock—bursting into flames." The plane dropped again and Marsha shuddered.

"It's going to be okay, Marsha," Allison said meekly. But Marsha's fear was contagious, and Allison felt herself beginning to succumb. She spoke to encourage herself as much as Marsha. "Don't worry, I heard the stewardess say we'd soon be out of it."

"Allison, at times like this I wonder about my life."

"What do you mean?" Allison looked at Marsha curiously.

"Oh, you know, I start to see myself for what I am, and I don't like it very much." Marsha looked down, still clinging to Allison's arm. "I'm pretty selfish. Don't look so surprised—you think I don't know it? I just figure it's my privilege."

Allison nodded, though she couldn't understand how anyone could hold such a high opinion of themselves.

"I think about people I've hurt along the way—I think about you, Allison, and your father . . ." The turbulence died down, and Marsha grew silent. Allison hated to lose this moment, but she could think of nothing more to say.

"Are you ladies okay?" the stewardess asked. "That should be the end of it—just a little storm over the mountains, that's all. Can I get you a drink, Miss Madison?"

"Yes," Marsha said, finally releasing Allison's arm. "I'll have a dry martini."

Allison sighed as the moment slipped away.

Eleven

"MARSHA," ALLISON WHISPERED as they approached Stanley in the New York air terminal. "Are you still my big sister as far as Stanley goes?"

Marsha laughed her light, tinkling movie-star laugh. "No, darling. Stanley knows all. I had to tell him when I got the telegram in Istanbul. He was very nice about the whole thing. But as far as the rest of the world goes—yes! Marsha Madison is certainly too young to have a grown daughter!"

Allison nodded and followed Marsha as she pressed a path to the pudgy little man in the dark pinstriped suit. Stanley was no handsome prince, but at least he appeared to genuinely care about his wife. He hugged Marsha and instructed his driver to pick up the bags.

"My sweet Marsha. I feel like it's been a year since I've seen you! These long-distance marriages are for the birds, but I've almost got everything wrapped up here. I have a little welcome-home gift for you." He produced a blue velvet box, and it reminded Allison of the old jewelry box her father had given Marsha so many years ago here in New York. Marsha must not have noticed the resemblance as she opened the box and squealed.

"Oh, Stanley, you're such a dear! It's just gorgeous, and I have the most exquisite gown to go with it!" She wrapped her arms around his neck and kissed him right there in the airport.

Allison looked around in embarrassment, then glanced into the open box clutched tightly in Marsha's gloved hand. A diamond and sapphire necklace sparkled against the plush blue velvet. Pretty, but Allison wondered if it was worth it. She mentally compared Stanley to her father. *How could Marsha have given Dad up so easily?* Allison pondered.

"Marie has fixed us a nice dinner at home, since I knew you'd be too exhausted to go out tonight. Was your flight all right, dear?"

Allison followed them to the taxi. It was like she was invisible. She wondered if they would even notice if she turned and walked the other direction.

"Stanley, it was simply horrible! The worst turbulence! I thought I'd never see you again!"

"Well, you're safe now, sweetheart." Stanley was speaking as if Marsha were a small child. "I will take care of you."

Allison rolled her eyes at the sticky sentiment and climbed into the car, wedging herself into a corner and hoping they'd continue to ignore her.

"Allison—forgive my manners. How are you?" Stanley asked, hardly looking at her.

"Fine."

"Good, good. Oh, Marsha, I almost forgot to tell you—"

Allison blocked out the rest of their conversation and focused instead on the New York skyline. The evening lights glittered and glowed and filled her with an odd sense of urgency. She didn't really like the big city. She'd never want to live here, especially after her visit at the beginning of the summer. That tiny bite out of the Big Apple had been overwhelming. Still, there was an indescribable something in the air. The twinkling city lights reminded her of Marsha's new necklace—shimmering with glitz and promising fulfillment, but empty and unable to deliver.

The penthouse looked exactly the same as when she'd left it. Allison chuckled to herself as she looked around and remembered how she'd made a mess of Marsha's apartment during her hideout in New York, then how she'd hurriedly cleaned up in fear of Lola dropping in. She went to the spare room—still cold and uninviting. She sat on the bed and the bedspread crackled just like it always did, only this time she didn't worry about the wrinkles. She opened the closet and discovered her bags. They must've been sent back from Camp Wannatonka when she hadn't show up. She didn't bother to unpack them. There wasn't anything she cared about in them anyway.

"Dinnertime, Allison," Marsha called.

They sat at the shiny black dining room table. The china was white, trimmed in black and gold and very elegant. Everything in Marsha's apartment was sleek and sophisticated, nothing cozy or homey. At least the Beverly Hills house was a little better, but nothing like her grandpa's house in Oregon.

"Allison, pass the salad, please," Marsha said in an irate voice, as if she'd asked once already. Allison passed the crystal bowl and picked at her dinner. She knew Marie was supposed to be a fantastic cook, but Allison didn't like French cooking. Everything was smothered with a thick white sauce and always tasted the same.

"Delicious dinner, Marie," Stanley said as he leaned back and lit a fat cigar. He stroked his hand across his shiny bald head and grinned at Marsha in satisfaction. "Yes, sirree, it's nice to have you back, Marsha old girl."

Marsha's eyes sparked with fire. "Old? What do you mean old?"

"Nothing at all, dear—just an expression, you know. After all, you're still my little girl." Stanley winked at her, but she continued to scowl. "How did negotiations go? Did you take them for their last penny, Marsha?"

"Humph! That studio is nuts! They offered me only half of what I should get!"

Stanley's jaw dropped. "What do you mean?"

"Just what I said! They made me a horrible offer!"

"Did you take it?"

"Yes. Lola said it was the best I'd get—" Marsha burst into tears and ran off to her bedroom. Stanley drummed his fingers on the table and nervously puffed his cigar.

"Excuse me," Allison whispered. He didn't even notice as she left the table. She flicked on the radio in her room and collapsed on the bed. Sweet strains of Nat King Cole drifted through her room, drowning out the heated discussion over finances that kept trying to slip beneath her closed door.

❧   ❧   ❧

The next morning Allison tiptoed out of her room and wandered through the empty apartment. She could hear Marie in the kitchen, softly singing along with the radio. Allison peeked in.

"You need something, *cherie*?" Marie asked in her thick French accent.

"No, not really," Allison said, starting to leave.

"You can come in—if you want. You like Hit Parade?"

"Yeah, I listen when I get the chance." Allison sat down on the kitchen stool and watched Marie whip eggs until they were fluffy.

"You like some tea?" Marie asked. Allison nodded and Marie poured her a cup. "I hear you go to court soon."

Allison looked up in surprise. "How did you know?"

"Oh, I'm sorry—I hear things. . . ."

Allison was curious. "Has Stanley been talking about the court case?"

"*Oui*, he and his lawyer friend discuss during dinner."

"How are things going on it?"

"Sounds good for them—is that not good for you, too?"

Allison sighed and stared at her tea.

"That's what I think. The way they talk—I think Allison is not people. You know—like you are dog or cat."

Allison laughed. "You have something there, Marie. What else did you hear?" Marie's face went blank when Marsha stepped in. Marsha frowned, and Marie turned and busied herself at the sink.

"Allison, it concerns me how much time you spend chatting with the hired help," Marsha said coolly. "It's not right. Maybe it was okay when you were a little girl, but I want you to stop it now."

Allison was stunned. How could Marsha talk like that in front of Marie—as if she weren't even there?

"Is breakfast ready, Marie? Allison, bring your tea out here. Stanley left already. He had some business to attend to."

Marie brought fluffy omelets and fresh squeezed orange juice to the table, and for a change Allison appreciated her culinary skills.

"I'd like to do some shopping while we're in New York, but I'm still exhausted from traveling. I plan to just relax and rest for the next couple days." Marsha's idle chatter did little to fill the uncomfortable silence.

Allison sipped her tea and wondered what she'd find to keep herself occupied during this time. Right now the adult world seemed pretty boring to her. She wondered what Andrew and Heather were doing, then realized they'd be in school. For once in her life she wished she could be in school, too. Even homework would be more interesting than this.

"I decided you shouldn't start school until this trial business is over, Allison," Marsha announced as if reading her thoughts. "I hope it won't be a problem."

"That's what I figured," Allison mumbled, trying to forget every dream she ever had about going to school with Heather in Oregon. Then, wondering what Marsha's school had been like, she asked, "Marsha, did you go to school in Cape Cod?"

Marsha looked across the room and thought for a moment. "Yes, it was a very small school. Mother wanted me to attend boarding school, but father insisted I stay at home."

"I can barely remember Grandfather Madison, but he seemed nice."

"In some ways he was. . . . When I was a girl, he was always occupied with business and wasn't home a lot. But we got along well until—" Marsha stopped and frowned.

"Until what?"

"Father didn't approve of acting. He felt it was beneath me." Marsha laughed, sounding hollow and empty.

"So what did he do?"

"In the beginning—when I was in high school—he thought it was okay. In fact, for the first time in my life he and Mother both paid a little attention to me. I liked that feeling of having them in the audience, clapping along with the rest of the community—all for me. I felt important and I wanted more. That's when the trouble began. . . ." Marsha poured another cup of tea and took a long, slow sip.

"My parents had a fit when I decided to go to New York for acting lessons. My father disowned me, but Mother sent me money behind his back. And it was fun. For the first time in my life, I was my own person—no one telling me what to do, how to hold a fork, or to mind my manners."

Allison smiled, knowing full well what that was like. "How

did you meet Dad?" She was treading on thin ice—but maybe it was her only chance.

"I met James at a small downtown gallery. I stopped in to get out of the rain, and I immediately noticed his impressionist paintings. They were so bright and cheerful and they reminded me of home—on the Cape. A handsome young man told me they were of the Oregon coast, clear across the country. I told him to tell the artist I admired his work, and he told me I just had. And we laughed." Marsha's face grew pale and her hand trembled on her teacup.

"Are you okay, Marsha?"

"Yes, it's just I've never told anyone these things and it's . . . difficult. He was very handsome and charming. He looked a lot like you, Allison."

"Did you love him?"

Marsha laughed again, this time in a sarcastic tone. "Love him? I adored him! And I worked hard to win him. I used every bait I could think of to hook him. He was just getting over some country girl in Oregon who'd jilted him, and I didn't waste any time."

Allison was surprised, for she'd always thought the opposite. It had never occurred to her that Marsha was the one who loved most in their relationship. "And your parents didn't approve?"

"Hardly! A penniless painter? They were mortified. This time Mother was even worse than Father. She cut off my allowance. Fortunately for me I was starting to get roles that paid well. But then you came along. I'm sorry, Allison, but I just wasn't ready to be a mother. That's when my parents stepped back into the picture. They found James a good job and took you back with them so you could have a normal childhood."

This time Allison laughed. "Normal?"

"Well, better than I could give you. James wanted to keep

you here. Can you imagine? A baby being raised by a struggling actress and fledgling artist in New York City? It would've been pitiful."

Allison wondered. Maybe it would've held them together. "What went wrong, Marsha?"

"Everything! Sometimes I wonder if he ever loved me. My career started to soar, and even though I was often gone, I brought in the money. James hated his job and kept trying to talk me into leaving New York and set up a real home—you know, with the white picket fence and all that. James resented my career, and I think that finally did it. That, along with the embezzlement scandal."

Allison was glad Marsha had brought it up. She took a deep breath. "But, Marsha, you knew all along he was innocent, didn't you?"

Marsha looked at her watch and feigned a yawn. "No, not really—I'm still not sure. I'm awfully tired now, Allison. We can talk more later." Marsha stood and slipped away to her room.

Allison sat at the table with fists clenched. She knew it was a lie. She'd already read the letter proclaiming her father's innocence. She wondered if Marsha even realized the letter was gone.

Marsha avoided Allison for the next couple days, staying mostly in her room or on the phone but always distant and aloof. Allison wrote more letters and some poetry and read a couple mindless novels from Stanley's collection.

One night Stanley and Marsha dressed up and went to an opening on Broadway. They hadn't asked Allison to join them, but she didn't care. It gave her time alone with Marie. Maybe she could pump her for information.

"Marie," Allison began as Marie cleared the table. "Have

you heard anything about the upcoming trial you could share with me?"

Marie looked flustered. "I am so sorry, cherie. Miss Madison, she warn me—I keep mouth closed now." Allison frowned. "But," Marie whispered as if the walls had ears, "I tell you this—you be careful."

That's all Marie would say, and Allison wondered what her warning could possibly mean. What did she need to be careful of? Obviously the court battle would be for her custody, but Allison wondered why Marsha would fight so hard for a daughter she never wanted in the first place. Was it only to get even with her father, or did Marsha actually, in her own warped way, truly love her?

Twelve

"MARSHA," STANLEY ANNOUNCED cheerily as he entered the apartment. "Your new script arrived." He opened his briefcase and held out a bulky parcel. "I picked it up in the lobby and sneaked a peek on my way up. It sounds intriguing. Care to take a look?"

For the first time in days, Marsha visibly perked up. Allison watched Marsha from the kitchen as she pored over the thick manuscript with guarded enthusiasm. Her face was a picture of emotion as she curled up on the couch in her white satin robe, quickly flipping from one page to the next. She giggled in spots like a young girl, and Allison sighed in relief to see Marsha at last regain an interest in something. Ever since their conversation about her father, Marsha had been quiet and depressed. Allison almost felt guilty for having brought it up.

"This is wonderful!" Marsha exclaimed. "It's sure to be a hit! I wonder if they've lined up my leading man yet. Hmm, who could it be?"

Stanley smiled smugly and patted Marsha's sleek, dark head. "It's a good thing I'm not given over to fits of jealousy, isn't it, darling?"

"Dear Stanley, what would I do without you?" She turned to Allison and smiled. "Say, I think it's about time for that shopping spree I promised you! Can you be ready by one? We'll do lunch, too! It's time New York got a good look at Marsha Madison again!"

Lunch was a lavish affair, but Allison actually enjoyed it,

especially after their recent days of seclusion in the penthouse. She made a point not to bring up any controversial topics, deciding it would be best not to upset Marsha just before the upcoming trial.

Marsha chattered away, mostly about herself and how she thought others perceived her. Allison was used to this self-absorbed gossip and didn't expect anything else these days. She listened complacently as they shopped, just happy to be out seeing people and things. As usual, Marsha insisted on buying items for Allison which she'd probably never wear, and Allison didn't bother to argue. Instead, she played the game, pretending they were the Madison sisters out on a buying spree.

They arrived home late in the afternoon, and Marsha retired to her bed in exhaustion. Allison ate a quiet dinner with Stanley. Then he picked up a cigar and his *Wall Street Journal* and disappeared to his room.

She went to her room and wrote a letter to her father. She didn't know if it would even get there in time, but it made her feel close to him. Writing had become a way of existence for her, and sometimes it was the only thing that made her feel alive. She figured she wrote an average of a letter a day, plus her journal and an occasional poem. It helped her to understand things better. She kept all her letters hidden beneath her bed in a large box tied with a yellow satin ribbon. Every night before she went to sleep she asked God to help her father win the custody trial. She didn't know if this prayer was fair to Marsha, but it was the only way she could pray sincerely. She remembered Constance had said when you pray to God you must be honest. For now, it was the best she could do.

❧   ❧   ❧

The day before the trial everyone was edgy, and Marsha

must have smoked a pack of cigarettes. Dinner was a silent meal, and even Marie seemed jumpy. Allison assumed she'd be allowed to attend the hearing but had been afraid to ask. As Marie served dessert, Allison mustered the boldness.

"Marsha, what should I wear tomorrow?" she asked, hoping to avoid the main conflict by discussing her courtroom attire.

"What—wear? What do you mean?"

"You know, for the trial. Should I wear a suit—"

"You won't need to go tomorrow," Marsha said sharply.

"I want to go. After all, this concerns *me*. I should get to be there." *How dare Marsha try to keep me away!* she fumed inwardly.

"Marsha," Stanley said. "Would it hurt for her to come? She's right, it does concern her."

Marsha grunted. "Oh, all right. I don't give a hoot! I'm so sick of this whole thing, I wish to heavens it were over!" She flung her napkin down and left the table.

Another wave of guilt rushed over Allison. She wished it were over, too. Sometimes she wondered if everyone would be happier if she'd never been born.

She went to her bedroom and laid out everything for the following day. She knew the trial was set for the morning and wanted to be ready. She looked out the window across the glittering skyline. *Dad must be in New York tonight*, she thought happily. *And Grace, too*. They had written that Grace would be staying with her Aunt Matilda on Long Island, and James would be holed up at the YMCA. It gave her hope that she'd be with them tomorrow. She repeated her prayer with an urgent expectancy, then tossed and turned all night, haunted by fragments of senseless nightmares.

ဆ   ဆ   ဆ

She awoke at the first light of day and carefully dressed. She put on the russet wool suit she'd selected on their last shopping spree. The stylish short jacket was trimmed in suede, and the long skirt cut full at the bottom with a lining that swished when she walked. She waited patiently in her room until she heard the others stirring and went out to find breakfast already laid on the table. She tried to eat but her stomach was knotted.

"Allison, pack some things to take to the Cape. We'll be going there right after the trial," Marsha announced curtly.

Allison quickly put some clothes into a bag. She wondered if she'd still have to go to Grandmother Madison's after her father won her custody at the trial. Well, at least she'd be ready to go home with him and have the rest of her stuff sent later. Marie smiled encouragingly at Allison and waved good-bye.

Marsha and Stanley rode in silence, and Allison watched out the window as people bustled along in and out of subways, scurrying like drones to work, oblivious to anyone's plight but their own.

They walked slowly up the steps to the courthouse and met Marsha's lawyer, Harrison Monroe. His black gabardine suit and smooth gray hair gave him a commanding image. He shook Allison's hand in a formal manner and escorted them to a windowless room inside the courthouse. There they sat in uncomfortable silence for almost an hour.

"Is this where the trial takes place?" Allison asked, looking around the small room.

"No, we just wait here until it's time for the hearing to begin," Mr. Monroe answered, thumbing through a small stack of paper work. He glanced at his pocket watch and snapped his briefcase closed. "Which is just about now. Everyone ready?"

They entered the courtroom and a pushy reporter asked Marsha questions, but she ignored him. The lawyer herded them down the aisle and Allison spotted her father and Grace straining to catch a glimpse of her across the crowded room. Instinctively she started for them, but Stanley grasped her firmly by the elbow and guided her to a chair. James winked and smiled, and she knew everything would be okay.

"All rise for the honorable Judge Emerson," the bailiff announced from the front of the room. The court came to order when the elderly judge approached the bench. He had a nice grandfatherly appearance. Most of the legal terminology and discussion sounded like mumbo jumbo to Allison, but when Marsha's attorney called James to the stand, she sat upright and listened closely.

"Now, Mr. O'Brian, you've come to request custody of Allison Mercury O'Brian. Is that correct?"

"Yes, sir," he answered.

"I have some questions regarding your fitness to assume this responsibility. First of all, what is your present occupation?"

"Well, actually, I'm an artist by trade, but I've only recently begun selling my work."

"And what did you do before that? Isn't it true you were a lighthouse keeper, living on a meager salary, barely sufficient to support yourself let alone a daughter?"

James frowned in perplexity. "Yes, but I—"

"Just answer the question, please."

"Yes."

"And before that you were employed in the U.S. Armed Forces?"

"That's correct."

"Not a very impressive résumé. . . . And before the army you were employed by National Insurance of New York?" The lawyer had an insinuating tone in his voice.

James smiled. "That's also correct."

"And what was the reason for your leaving National?"

"I was accused of embezzlement, but—"

"Embezzlement?" He said the word with dramatic emphasis. "Were charges filed against you?"

"Yes, but I went into the service and to my knowledge they were dropped."

"To your knowledge? Are you certain they were dropped?"

"No, but I have proof of my innocence."

Mr. Monroe's face momentarily registered surprise, then he changed his line of questioning altogether. "Are you a single man, Mr. O'Brian?"

"Yes, but—"

"Just answer the questions, please. Do you think a single man is the best sort of parent for an adolescent girl?"

"Well, no, not really, but I plan to—"

"Please, Mr. O'Brian—just answer the question."

Allison felt like screaming. Why didn't they let him talk? How dare they treat him in such a way! She glared angrily at Marsha and Stanley while they both watched in fascination as Mr. Monroe continued to grill and twist, making James O'Brian look like the most unfit parent ever to walk the face of the earth. James' face grew red, and she wondered if he wanted to explode as much as she did.

Finally, Mr. Monroe smiled and folded his arms. "No more questions, thank you. I now call Marsha Madison to the stand." He asked Marsha about her income stability and Allison's schooling, attempting to make Marsha sound like a loving and responsible parent. And if Allison could've erased the last fourteen years of neglect, she'd have almost believed him, too.

"Miss Madison, how long has it been since the divorce?"

"About seven years."

"I'm sorry to bring up such an emotional subject," Monroe

apologized as Marsha reached for a handkerchief. "May I ask what brought about your divorce?"

"There were a lot of problems, but when James was accused of embezzlement—it was just the last straw—"

"That's a lie!" James rose to his feet but was pulled back by his lawyer.

"Order!" yelled the judge, pounding his gavel loudly. "Mr. O'Brian, I will not tolerate these outbursts."

"Miss Madison," said Mr. Monroe kindly. "Has your ex-husband ever offered to pay child support for Allison?"

"No, he has not." Marsha looked directly at James, then quickly turned away.

"So you have virtually supported your daughter for most of her life—provided her food, shelter, clothing, and education, I might add, at one of the finest private schools on the East Coast. And then her father pops in out of the blue and wants to take her away. That must be very upsetting and distressful to you."

"Objection," James' lawyer cried. "Miss Madison's personal feelings have no bearing on this case."

"Sustained."

"Thank you, Miss Madison, that's all I have," Mr. Monroe said, taking her hand and helping her from the stand. Mr. Monroe made a brief speech about Marsha's love and devotion for Allison and finally sat down. Allison glared at him in disgust.

James was called to the stand again, but this time it was from his own lawyer, Aaron Weirs. Allison smiled at him and his jaw relaxed a little.

"Mr. O'Brian," Mr. Weirs began in a soft tone. "Please tell us why your wife divorced you." Marsha squirmed slightly next to Allison.

James looked straight at Marsha and said, "Our marriage

had been rocky from the start, but I always figured in time we'd work it out. But I believe the real reason Marsha filed was because she was having an affair with her director—"

"Objection!" Mr. Monroe yelled. "That is only Mr. O'Brian's speculation, not a fact."

"Sustained. Stick to the facts, Mr. O'Brian."

"Were Miss Madison's accusations regarding the embezzlement charges from National Insurance of New York true?" Mr. Weirs asked.

"No, the charges were completely without proof. I have given you a letter that has been substantiated to verify my innocence."

Marsha looked at her lawyer in surprise as Mr. Weirs presented the documents to the judge as evidence.

"And why have you spent the last few years as a lighthouse keeper?"

"It's hard to explain," James began. "After the war, I felt my life was over, and I was diagnosed with what they call shell shock. The embezzlement charges had ruined my reputation, and Marsha had made sure I would never get to see my daughter. Life was so hopeless, some days I hardly had the strength to go on. But I spent time painting and thinking as I worked at the lighthouse, hoping one day my name would be cleared and I could resume life—maybe even see Allison."

"Do you have any idea who framed you in these charges?"

"Yes, we know almost for certain it was Marsha—"

"Objection!" Mr. Monroe yelled again. "This is purely speculation and not allowable in this court!"

"Sustained. Once again I must insist—please stick to the facts!"

Mr. Weirs nodded to the judge and went on. "Mr. O'Brian, how did Allison come to be in Oregon?"

"My father, before he passed away, had written Marsha many times begging her to allow Allison a visit. Allison had no idea she even had a grandfather in Oregon. When she found out, she came out to meet him. Unfortunately, she came without her mother's permission. Of course her mother, as usual, was far away and out of touch—"

"Objection!"

"Your honor, how can I answer the questions if Mr. Monroe keeps interrupting?" James asked in an irritated voice.

The judge scowled. "Just answer the questions."

"Mr. O'Brian, what are your plans if you attain Allison's custody?"

"Right now I am financially stable, and I have a home for her. I plan to continue my art, and there's a wedding in my future." He smiled across the room to Grace, and Allison felt Marsha bristle. "Allison would attend the local high school and enjoy a normal life for a change—"

"Objection!"

"I'm finished with my questions. You may step down, Mr. O'Brian." Mr. Weirs smiled at James. "I'd like to call Miss Madison to the stand."

After some preliminary questions, Mr. Weirs jumped right in. "Miss Madison, how many times have you been married?"

"Three," she mumbled.

"Three?" he repeated loudly. "And do you think your present marriage will last?"

"Objection!"

"Your honor," Mr. Weirs argued. "I'm trying to establish a pattern for Allison's future." The judge nodded grimly. "Miss Madison?"

"Well, of course," Marsha snapped.

"But with your history, wouldn't you think it's possible this marriage might—"

"Objection. He's badgering the witness."

"Okay, let me ask another question," Mr. Weirs said. "Miss Madison, do you think you provide a stable home environment for your daughter?"

"Well, it's been difficult. I just bought a home in California, and Allison has been staying there with me. I think she likes it—"

"So you plan to keep her there while you're off making movies?"

"Allison is a big girl. She doesn't need her mommy to hold her hand!"

"Have you ever held her hand?"

Marsha stared blankly and Mr. Weirs continued.

"Isn't it true she doesn't even call you Mother, you hardly ever spend time with her, and she spends the school year in boarding school and summers at camps?" Mr. Monroe's objections became lost in between Mr. Weirs' loud questions and the uproar of the audience.

The judge pounded his gavel and yelled, "Order! I demand order!" He looked sternly at Mr. Weirs. "I'm warning you one last time!"

"Thank you, your honor, I'm finished with Miss Madison."

"I adjourn this court to a short recess," the judge proclaimed. "We'll meet back here at twelve-thirty for my decision."

Marsha and Stanley followed Mr. Monroe, almost dragging Allison from the courtroom.

"I want to see my dad!" she exclaimed.

"Not now!" Marsha hissed.

Allison sulked through a quick lunch, barely touching her sandwich. No one seemed to notice. Marsha didn't order any food, instead she chain-smoked and nervously sipped a martini. Only Stanley had an appetite, and he disappeared behind his *Wall Street Journal* as soon as he finished his prime rib. Allison stared at Marsha, but Marsha wouldn't look her way. She kept glancing at her watch and snapping her gold cigarette case open and shut, over and over. Just when Allison thought she might scream, Marsha announced it was time to return to the court-house.

On the way back, Allison consoled herself with the fact that her father's testimony was convincing. It sounded more like he really cared for Allison. And at least he'd cleared his name, even if they wouldn't allow him to use it as evidence against Marsha. She silently prayed and crossed her fingers for luck.

It seemed even more news people and photographers were there as they pressed their way into the courtroom. Allison knew it was because of Marsha and wished they'd all leave them alone. Lights flashed in her face, and a reporter grabbed her by the sleeve. "Allison O'Brian? Is it true that Marsha Madison is really your mother? Who do you want to live with, your mom or your dad—"

"No comment!" Stanley yelled right in the reporter's face.

They pushed their way to their seats and quickly sat down. The room was buzzing with excitement, and Allison's heart pounded in her ears. She closed her eyes, willing herself to be calm and brave. When she opened them again, the judge sat sternly at the front of the court while he shuffled his papers. Feeling like a criminal about to be sentenced, she fought a wave of nausea and waited for his decision.

Thirteen

"THESE ARE MY LEAST FAVORITE of all court hearings," the judge began in a solemn voice. "And although it isn't easy, I try to make decisions that are just and in the best interest of everyone." He cleared his throat and Allison wished he'd get to it. She peeked over at her father and saw him smile at her.

"In the case of Allison Mercury O'Brian, she is a lucky child to have two parents who love her so and want to take care of her. But I have decided in this case, and in the case of so many others, that a child is usually best left in the hands of the mother—"

No, it can't be true, she cried inwardly. *There must be some kind of mistake*. She looked over at Marsha and saw a smile of satisfaction spread across her face. "Don't you care about what I want?" Allison screamed, but her voice was nearly lost in the courtroom noise, and the gavel came down with a resounding crash.

"Order! Order!" The judge looked directly at Allison and she hoped he was going to allow her to speak, but instead he continued. "As I was saying, I have decided to allow Marsha Madison to continue in the care and custody of Allison Mercury O'Brian. I do suggest, for the sake of the child, that some sort of visitation schedule be arranged between both parents and their legal counsel." He pounded his gavel and adjourned the court, leaving through a little door in the back.

Allison wanted to follow him and demand that he hear her side. What right had he to decide? Her head began to swim and tears blurred her eyes. She sat down and put her hands over her face. Was this God's answer to her prayers? She couldn't believe it! All around her, Marsha's friends and acquaintances were shaking hands and congratulating Marsha.

"She'll be okay," Marsha said. "It's been so difficult on her— I'm so glad this is all over. Now we can get on with our lives, or at least try to." Marsha groaned, then said quietly to Stanley, "In moments, the whole world will know that Marsha Madison has a daughter!"

Allison suddenly remembered her father. She stood and looked and saw him at the table with his head bowed down in his hands. Grace sat at his side with tears streaming down her face. Allison slipped through the crowd almost unnoticed.

"Dad," she began, then choked. He stood and hugged her.

"I'm so sorry, Allison. I'm so sorry. I don't know what went wrong. I can't believe it! I thought for sure the judge would see—"

"Hello, James," Marsha said coolly from behind Allison. "No reason for us to act uncivilized now, is there? I'm sorry for your disappointment, but like the judge said, maybe we can arrange a visitation schedule. I'm not one to be unreasonable, you know."

James' jaw twitched in anger. "What did you have in mind, Marsha? Two weeks every summer?"

"Oh, I'm sure we can work out something—something that will make everyone happy. Look, James, we're going up to the Cape right now. Why don't you and your friend come on out and join us, and we'll work something out. I really think for Allison's sake it's time to bury the hatchet and be civilized adults. Don't you?" She extended her hand in truce. James scowled and looked at her suspiciously, then over to Allison. Allison forced a smile and shrugged, and James halfheartedly shook Marsha's hand.

"Fine," Marsha said. "We're leaving right away. We'll see you later tonight, then?"

"Are you sure your mother wants our company?" James asked. "You know she's never welcomed me before."

"James, you of all people should know to never take Mother too seriously." Marsha smiled in that funny way and poked James in the arm, almost in a flirtatious manner.

❧ ❧ ❧

"I brought along a bottle of champagne to celebrate our victory," Stanley announced as they climbed into the limousine.

"And what made you so sure we'd need it?" Marsha asked lightly.

"Oh, just a wild guess."

Allison tried to ignore them while they joked and laughed like a couple of giddy kids, all the gaiety at her expense. She couldn't believe they'd be her parents from now on.

Late in the afternoon, they stopped for dinner at a lobster house in Rhode Island. Allison ate quickly and returned to the car. She curled up in a corner and closed her eyes, pretending it was all just a bad dream and she'd wake up in Oregon.

"Allison, we're here," Marsha said.

It was dark out, and Allison stumbled from the car and into the brightly lit house. She immediately recognized the polished green marble floor in the entry of Grandmother Madison's sprawling mansion. Gerald, the old butler, met them solemnly at the door.

"Mrs. Madison has retired for the evening, but I'll show you to your rooms." Allison followed as Marsha and Stanley were led down the north hall, then Gerald took her to a guest room in the west wing. She'd never stayed in a guest room here before. Grandmother usually put her in her old bed up in the nursery, which suited her just fine.

"Are you sure Grandmother wants me in here?" Allison asked, looking around the room. Gerald nodded. Allison shook her head and set her suitcase by the big four-poster bed. It was odd being treated like a guest. Usually she felt like excess baggage, always in the way as far as Grandmother Madison was concerned. Could there be hope for this side of her family after all?

Allison slipped down the stairs and into the drawing room that overlooked the driveway. She wanted to keep watch for when Dad and Grace came. She hoped they wouldn't change their minds. It might be her only chance to see them before . . . She wouldn't allow herself to think about that. She didn't want to accept the outcome of the trial yet. She stared blankly out the window. All was dark outside. The main road couldn't be seen from here, but she kept imagining them driving up in a rented car. She'd rush out and greet them.

When it was well after midnight and there was still no sign of them, she tiptoed back to bed. The sheets were like ice and she shivered. Tears of frustration slid down her cheeks, and out of habit she began to pray just like she'd done each night since camp. She'd always prayed to live with her dad at Tamaqua Point, but she couldn't pray that anymore. God hadn't answered her prayers, so why should she ask Him for anything else? She rolled over in anger and wept.

☙　☙　☙

The next morning dawned, and for the first time in her life she didn't want to get up. She didn't want to see Grandmother Madison or Stanley's and Marsha's triumphant faces. She trudged downstairs quietly and slipped out a side door and into the garden. The flowers had already started to die, and a crisp breeze blew off the Atlantic. She sat down on a bench and stared at the large stone house. Grandpa's house in Oregon was stone, too, but his had such an interesting shape. Grandmother Madison's was just long and sprawling, with dozens of high windows staring blankly across the grounds like empty eyes. She knew it had been in the Madison family for generations, but she'd never belonged here and didn't want to now.

A horn honked in the driveway, and she looked up to see an arm waving from the window of a bright yellow car. It was Grace and Dad. She dashed over to them.

"I thought you weren't coming!" she yelled.

"We decided not to come last night because it was getting so late. But even an army of Grandmother Madisons couldn't keep me away from you anymore." James laughed with a trace of sadness still in his eyes.

"Thank you for coming. I was afraid I wouldn't see you again! Come on—have you had breakfast?" Allison hopped in and rode with them up the driveway, then happily led them into the dining room as if she owned the house herself. Let Grandmother Madison fuss and fume, she didn't care.

"Hello, Grandmother," Allison announced lightly to the staunch old woman at the head of the table. "We have two guests for breakfast. Of course, you already know my dad. And this is my friend Grace. Grace, this is Mrs. Madison."

For a change Grandmother's acidic tongue was speechless. She just blinked and motioned to the empty chairs, not bothering to rise.

A maid Allison had never met served them eggs and sausage without batting an eyelash, as if people always dropped in out of the blue for breakfast.

"Did you have a good drive?" Allison asked, taking the role of hostess.

"It was lovely, Allison," Grace said. "Such a nice stretch of coast. It's different from the West Coast. And you have a simply beautiful place here, Mrs. Madison."

"Thank you," Grandmother Madison said stiffly.

"It was so hospitable of you to have us, and on such short notice."

Grandmother Madison grunted without even looking up from her egg cup. Allison felt embarrassed by her grandmother's lack of manners. This was the same grandmother who'd always lectured on things like etiquette, protocol, and good breeding.

"If you'd like, I could show you around the place after breakfast," Allison offered. Grandmother Madison ignored her, but Allison didn't care. "There's a neat carriage house with some old buggies, and the stables are really nice. Grandfather Madison used to have lots of race horses—I can barely remember, but they were pretty. I think there are still a couple horses around."

They finished breakfast and Allison quickly scooted them outside, thankful Marsha and Stanley weren't up yet. "Phew," Allison breathed as soon as they were on their way to the carriage house. "It was a little too stuffy in there for me—if you know what I mean."

Allison opened the door to the carriage house. Inside were old cars and buggies, a pot-bellied stove, and a few ancient easy chairs gathered around. Allison held her hands over the crackling stove.

"Looks like Harmon has already been here this morning. He's the caretaker. This used to be Grandfather Madison's favorite getaway—I think he used to run away from Grandmother Madison in here. I suppose Harmon mostly uses it now."

They all sat down in the chairs, and Allison studied them

both. Their faces looked tired and sad, and she knew it was due to her.

James rubbed his hands over the stove and stared at the harnesses hanging on the wall. Allison leaned back and breathed in the pungent smell of the musty room. It always reminded her of when she was a tiny girl. Grandfather Madison used to bring her in here while he smoked his pipe and read the paper. She would play with a big box of harness rings and odd pieces of shiny metal.

"I haven't given up, Allison. I still have a plan," James said with conviction in his eyes. "I want to appeal yesterday's decision. My lawyer has suggested I sue Marsha for defamation of character, and I think if I fight hard enough, I can win." His jaw grew firm, and he punched his fist into his open palm like a boxer getting ready for the fight.

Allison looked over to Grace. Her head hung sadly, and Allison wondered what Grace thought of his plan. "How long do you think it'll take?" she asked.

"Well, my lawyer thinks realistically it'll be nearly a year before we gather enough evidence to take it to court."

"And what will you do during that time? Are you . . . will you be getting, you know . . . married?" Allison didn't know how to ask. Grace looked up and started to say something, but James cut her off.

"We do plan to marry. But I would have to stay in New York awhile to do some research." Grace's face grew grim, and Allison knew she was worried.

"What do you think of all this, Grace?" Allison asked.

"Allison, you know I want whatever it takes to get you back home with us—if that's what you really want. I have to admit it would be hard seeing James stay in New York. That's where I lost him in the first place. . . ." Her voice trailed off.

"Dad, do you realize by the time it goes to court I'd be nearly sixteen. Marsha only has custody of me until I'm eighteen. Is it really worth it to go through all this?" It made her miserable to think of Grace and Dad and how they'd be putting their lives on hold for her—not to mention Andrew, Heather, and Winston. Allison knew in her heart they should be a family. Grace needed Dad right now, probably even more than Allison did.

"Allison, it'd still be worth it," James argued. "You are my only flesh and blood. You belong with me. Don't you want to live with us in Oregon?"

Allison looked down at the bleached floorboards polished smooth over the years. "I don't know . . . I don't know if it's worth it," she lied.

"What? Do you mean it? Allison, after all you went through to stay in Oregon—you don't think it's worth it?" James ran his fingers through his hair and stood. Allison couldn't look at him, and he paced back and forth across the shadowy room.

"It's not that I don't love you," she began. "But maybe we should just try to make the best of it. Marsha sounds willing to let me visit you. And Los Angeles isn't all that far away. . . ."

"Do you really want that, Allison? Do you really want me to give up?" He looked straight into her face and she nodded. Tears filled her eyes and she knew it was a lie, but she was tired of ruining other people's lives. James shook his head in disbelief and collapsed into the chair.

Grace leaned forward and placed a hand on his knee. "James, you never stopped to consider that Allison may have feelings for Marsha, too. They spent a lot of time together this summer—remember the letters? I think this is the closest Allison has ever been to her mother."

"Is that true, Allison?" James asked. "Because no matter what I think of Marsha, I wouldn't try to come between you two if I believed it's what you really wanted."

"I think it's best," Allison said quietly.

James walked over to a dusty window and looked out across the grounds. "Well, I have to admit, Allison, you do have quite a heritage here. The Madisons of Massachusetts are an influential family. You'll never go without. I certainly can't compete with their wealth, nor Marsha's fame. . . ."

Allison wanted to die. It was as if she'd knifed him in the back and twisted it. "Dad," she cried, "I will always love you!"

He held her in a tight grip. "I know, Allison. You'll have to forgive me. I guess I'm just jealous. I'm sorry."

"And we'll work it out so I can visit you a lot!" Allison exclaimed.

"Hello in there!" Marsha called. She walked into the carriage house. "I hope I'm not interrupting anything. I've been looking all over for you. I heard Allison was giving tours this morning. Have you seen it all yet?"

"Not everything," Grace said.

"Well, you must allow me to help show our guests around. Do you mind, Allison?" Marsha linked arms with Grace and led the way, explaining dates and history as she went. James and Allison followed silently in joint amazement.

"How long can you stay?" Allison whispered.

"Only for the day. We need to get back in time for our tickets. I had reserved a ticket for you, too, Allison."

Allison swallowed the gigantic lump in her throat. "How does Heather like high school, Dad?" Her voice sounded twisted and strange.

"Oh, it's going super!" James brightened up. "That girl has courage, Allison. She's already first flute chair in orchestra—of course, that's no surprise. But she misses you something terrible."

"I miss her, too. Do you think she could come visit me in California? And you and Grace, too—I mean, if you want."

"Sure, if we can work it out. I wonder if Marsha would let you spend Christmas in Oregon?"

"I hope so, Dad."

James smiled and squeezed Allison's arm. "Maybe everything will be okay, Allison. If you're happy, I'll try to be happy, too."

"Grace tells me you can only stay for the day, James," Marsha said, leading them into the house. "I'm sorry it has to be so short."

"Maybe we should get down to business, then," James said in a cool tone. "I'd like a written agreement about visitation for Allison."

"Well, you aren't much fun, James. You know what they say, all work and no play—"

"I didn't come to play, Marsha."

"I gathered that, James. Let's go into Daddy's library. We might find some paper and pens in there. That is unless you want me to sign it in blood." Marsha laughed at her joke.

"I don't think it would make much difference one way or the other," James seethed.

"Aren't we a little testy this morning," Marsha teased. Allison watched her father's face grow red and wondered how much he could take.

Marsha sat behind the large dark desk and pulled open a drawer. "Let's see . . . where do we begin?" she asked, poising a gold pen in the air.

"How about holidays?" Grace suggested. "Maybe Allison could come up for Christmas and Easter?"

"Hmm, I don't know," Marsha murmured. "I was thinking more along the line of a week or two each summer—"

"I knew it!" James exploded. "Forget it! I won't settle for a week or two each summer, Marsha. You'll have to do better than that!"

"Let's not get all heated up, James," Marsha said with a smile. "We won't accomplish anything like that. Okay, maybe she could come for Christmas vacation—"

Allison stood up and wanted to scream, but instead she walked out and slammed the door. It was more than she could bear to sit silently while they discussed her as if she were a dog, being shared back and forth like that. Grace followed her.

"Allison, I know it's difficult for you," Grace began.

"I just can't take it, Grace. Sometimes it feels like I'm not even a person—just a thing."

"I can guarantee your father does not see you as a thing. He loves you dearly, and he will fight for you, Allison—if you want him to. You just say the word. But if you want to be with Marsha, he'll back down. You're the only one who knows what you really want."

"I know," Allison said. But what she wanted would only complicate life for everyone. "Grace, when do you think you'll get married?"

"I really haven't given it much thought, Allison. We want you to be there, of course. Maybe if you get to come at Christmas we could plan something then."

"That would be nice." Why didn't she believe her own words?

"Excuse me," the butler interrupted. "Mrs. Madison wants to know if Mr. O'Brian and his friend will be staying for lunch."

"You are staying, aren't you?" Allison begged.

"Sure, we'd love to. But we'll have to leave soon after in order to catch our train."

Lunch was a solemn affair. Grandmother Madison said

about eight words altogether, though Marsha and Stanley tried amazingly hard to be polite. Allison couldn't bring herself to engage in chitchat while she witnessed her world evaporating before her eyes.

She stood out on the driveway with James and Grace, searching for the right words and staring at the hood of the car. The lump in her throat ached as she hugged them good-bye.

"Allison, I'll write you as often as I can," James promised, his eyes red. "And I'll see if I can arrange an exhibit down in California—then I'll have a double excuse to visit. You write or call if you need anything, you hear?" He kissed her on the cheek, and she tried to memorize the clean smell of his aftershave.

She gulped and nodded, then waved as the car moved slowly down the driveway. The bright yellow sedan became a blurry blob. The visitation schedule had been agreed upon, and Marsha had really been quite fair. Allison knew she should be thankful. She would have both Christmas and Easter vacations, plus one whole month in the summer to spend in Oregon. But it just wasn't enough. Allison dashed up to her room to sob in private.

Fourteen

ALLISON SCOLDED HERSELF for being so childish. Why cry now? It wasn't as if her world had changed all that much since last spring. If anything, she had a lot to be thankful for. First, she'd enjoyed a brief time of getting acquainted with Grandpa in Oregon. Then she'd discovered her father was still alive. She'd made some new friends, and now for the first time she was developing a relationship with her own mother. Besides, living in Beverly Hills wouldn't be all bad. There was Gertie and Adam; they'd be happy to see her again. And Christmas wasn't too far off.

She walked downstairs with determination to look at the bright side—just the way she'd seen Heather and Grace do. Marsha met her on the landing.

"So the lovebirds got off okay?" Marsha asked.

Allison rolled her eyes. "Yeah, about an hour ago."

"You need to get ready, too, Allison. You'll be leaving tomorrow morning at eight," Marsha announced nonchalantly. Her eyes didn't meet Allison's; instead, she studied a sharp red fingernail with total absorption.

"Leaving to where? Back to Los Angeles already?"

"No. Back to Oakmont Academy. It's all been arranged—"

"What? What do you mean? I thought I was going to live with you in Beverly Hills!" Allison could hear her own voice echoing down the hall, shrill and desperate.

"For heaven's sake, Allison, don't have a fit! You know I'll be

busy working on my new film. I won't have time to take care of
you—"

"Then why did you fight so hard to keep me?"

"Oh, Allison, don't get all worked up. It's no big deal—you'll
be back with your friends at the academy. What's so bad about
that?"

"Oh, nothing!" Allison answered sarcastically. "Nothing at
all. I just love staying in drafty dorms all my life with a bunch
of snotty girls! Especially when I could've lived with my own
dad, been with my own friends, and gone to a *real* high school.
No, Marsha, I'm just thrilled about this! Can't you tell?" Allison
felt close to hysterics. So much for positive thinking.

"Get used to it, Allison! The judge gave *me* custody—*not*
your father. Don't forget it!"

Allison stomped up the stairs and flopped across her bed.
How could Marsha be so unfeeling, so unfair? What would that
judge think now? Did he have any idea what his decision had
cost her? And what in the world had given Marsha this sudden
change of attitude? Maybe this was Grandmother Madison's
doing. After all, Marsha and Allison had almost become friends
these past few weeks. Allison had to make Marsha understand
how important it was for her to at least be in California with
her.

Allison quietly slipped back downstairs in search of Marsha.
She heard voices floating up the main hall, and just as she approached the drawing room entry she hesitated. Allison ducked
into a corner behind a Greek statue of a woman with a water
pitcher. The carved figure teetered slightly, and Allison steadied
it with her shaking hand, then listened through the open door
of the drawing room.

"Mother, I had no idea it would be so easy, but once again
you were right! Really, I should get an Academy Award for my

fantastic performance. I had them all convinced! Even James believed me in the end." Marsha laughed loudly, and Allison's fingers grew cold upon the statue's head.

"Well, Marsha, your acting abilities have finally paid off for me. I don't know what we'd have done if James had won that custody suit. One thing's for certain, Allison's inheritance would have come out into the open, and who knows what that good-for-nothing James might have done about it."

"I still don't know why Daddy went and did that, Mother," Marsha complained. "Was it just to spite me—did he despise me that much? That he would go and make Allison the sole heiress of the entire Madison estate! Was it just to teach me a lesson?"

Allison gasped in disbelief. Could it be true? Was this whole place really hers? She stared down the hall of the grand mansion in momentary astonishment, trying to take in the meaning of those words. She was an heiress. But with a force of its own, the awful realization struck her. Marsha's affection toward her had been nothing more than an act—a complete farce! Her mother's dramatic talents had been put to work to secure the family fortune a little longer! Allison seethed inwardly, and angry tears burned in her eyes as she continued to eavesdrop without guilt.

"Your father was an odd man," Grandmother Madison said with a loud sigh. "He was extremely old-fashioned about most things but in some ways very unconventional. It was as if his wealth meant absolutely nothing to him. Sometimes I'd catch him giving away vast sums of money to charitable organizations." She gasped dramatically as if compassion were a disgrace. "You'd think he wanted to put us all in the poorhouse! Can you imagine anything so completely absurd?"

"Well, Mother, I'm glad you're happy now. But you know, the

time will still come when Allison will find out. Have you discussed this with your lawyers yet?"

"Of course, and so far they've come up empty-handed. We'll keep it a secret as long as possible. I've transferred much into your name already, Marsha, but I'm trying to be discreet. Unfortunately, my hands are tied when it comes to the estate. But at least for now we've kept it out of James O'Brian's lap." Their laughter echoed down the hall, and their footsteps approached the open door.

Allison scurried around the corner and out the side door through the garden. She ran down a rosebush-lined trail, shaking her head in wonder as if that somehow might sift her jumbled thoughts. A stiff sea breeze stripped petals from wilted blooms and swirled them across the path before her in a blur of faded pink and red. Cutting across the east lawn, she searched for the old gap in the tall thicket hedge that surrounded the estate. There it was, but now only a slight gaping hole remained. She knelt down and squeezed through, then headed toward the sea.

The breeze picked up by the shore and whipped her blouse, making it snap and crackle in the wind. She walked along the top of the familiar rocky cliffs, almost without seeing. The surf pounded and crashed below her, but it couldn't drown the sound of the pain screaming inside her brain. The ocean's thrashing seemed mild compared to her battered emotions.

How could Marsha be so heartless and cruel? To fight for Allison not because she wanted her but to protect and secure Grandmother Madison's fortune—as if Allison cared about it in the first place. Allison's mind spun ornate plans of revenge that only tumbled into muddled confusion and ended in hopelessness.

"I hate you, Marsha Madison!" she screamed at the sea, but

her words were swallowed by the wind. "I hate you, and I'll never forgive you for what you've done to me! I hate you, I hate you, I hate you!" She collapsed on the edge of the bluff and broke into uncontrollable sobs. Sprays of mist shot into the air above her and floated down upon her back like ice-cold fingers. She peered down over the edge of the cliff, watching the breakers smash wickedly onto the rocks below. They reached up as if to tease and taunt her, saying, *You lose, Allison! You lose!*

Then she heard another voice. It was quiet as a feather on the breeze but louder than the bashing waves upon the rocks. "Forgive her" was all it said.

Allison looked around in surprise. The voice came again, clearer this time. "Forgive her."

Allison pressed her hands over her ears, trying to smother the voice that was speaking within her own soul. She remembered Constance's talk about forgiving her alcoholic father. She remembered the letter Constance had sent. But Allison didn't want to forgive Marsha. Marsha didn't deserve to be forgiven.

Allison stood and stared down the side of the cliff, and the vision before her blurred and swirled. The unsteady surface beneath her feet was wet and slick. Her father's anguished face flashed through her mind with startling clarity, his eyes pleading with her, begging her to step back. Cautiously, she inched from the ledge and away from danger. She backed up until she bumped into a large boulder jutting out from the bluff. She leaned into its solidness and shuddered.

Wedged into the cleft of the wet rock, she wrapped her arms around her middle and sobbed. They were no longer angry tears but the tears of a disillusioned and broken heart.

She remembered crying out to God not so very long ago. It was on a rocky island on the other side of the country. But she'd asked Him for help and He'd delivered. Still, she'd never really given her life to God, not like she'd meant to. Now she had nothing left to cling to. She felt hopelessly alone. Constance had explained how Allison must surrender all. Finally she understood.

"Dear God," she whispered. "You can have my life—all of it. There's nothing I can do with it, anyway. Please, God, just take it. I give it to you." She looked out across the ocean at the thick gray clouds piled across the horizon. How she longed for them to open and expose a beam of sunlight or a rainbow of promise. Instead, she felt the promise being etched on her heart with startling precision. She sighed and whispered a humble thanks.

She could finally accept that Marsha didn't love her and never really had. Perhaps in Marsha's own broken way she cared for Allison a little, but she would never be the kind of mother she needed. For once, Allison felt truly sorry for Marsha. What kind of life would it be to love no one . . . and perhaps to be loved by no one. Even Marsha's closest friends didn't seem to genuinely care for her. They respected her position in life, or maybe it was just her money. And at times when Stanley became angry over finances, Allison worried that he'd only married Marsha for her money and fame. Poor Marsha.

Suddenly, Allison realized she'd forgiven Marsha—just like that! Of course, it wasn't her own doing. No, like with Constance, this was a miracle. She felt free. She breathed deeply the sea air, then shivered. She was cold and wet, and she knew she should get back.

She slipped up to her room unnoticed and quickly changed into dry clothes, then packed her bags, like Marsha had told her. She didn't want to return to Oakmont, but then she knew she had no alternatives. Allison was about to pack her journal on top of her suitcase, but instead she opened it and began a poem. Her pen sprinted across the lined page as if self-propelled.

Heritage of Love

Dear Marsha, or Mother, whoever you are,
I shall no longer wish upon a star
For your love is elusive and vain,
And it has caused me too much pain.
Instead, I shall extend to you
My unfettered love, real and true.
It's all I have and I freely give.
I only ask that you'll let me live
Without deception or cruel lies—
It's there, I see it in your eyes.
All I ask is please be fair,
If it's possible that you care,
And listen to your child's plea
And open your eyes so you can see,
Your riches and wealth mean nothing to me!
I'd give my inheritance just to be free
To live and to love, free from strife
In a home with my dad and a real life.
And I'd still love you, though from afar
But I wouldn't be a butterfly trapped in a jar.
I'd gladly give up this entire estate
If only to secure a happier fate.

She ripped the poem out of her journal and stared at it. Without waiting a moment longer, she wrote on the bottom of the page, "Marsha, I *would* give back to you the entire Madison estate if I could only be free. If you would just let me go to my dad, I would never ask for a single penny."

She slipped the poem in an envelope, then tiptoed down the hallway. Marsha's door was closed, but Allison could hear movement inside. She took a deep breath, then slid it under the door. With clenched teeth, she stepped back and stared at the closed door before her. Was there any hope that Marsha would change her mind and allow her to return to Oregon? Allison closed her eyes and breathed a silent prayer. It was in God's hands now.

∞   ∞   ∞

Allison is nervously awaiting her mother's response to her desperate request. She knows this is her last chance to make Marsha see how much she wants to live with her father. Will Marsha finally understand what Allison has been trying to show her all along, or will she force Allison to live a life apart from the ones who truly love her? Find out in THE ALLISON CHRONICLES #3.

Teen Series From
Bethany House Publishers

Early Teen Fiction (11–14)

THE ALLISON CHRONICLES by Melody Carlson
Follow along as Allison O'Brian, the daughter of a famous 1940s movie star, searches for the truth about her past and the love of a family.

HIGH HURDLES by Lauraine Snelling
Show jumper DJ Randall strives to defy the odds and achieve her dream of winning Olympic Gold.

SUMMERHILL SECRETS by Beverly Lewis
Fun-loving Merry Hanson encounters mystery and excitement in Pennsylvania's Amish country.

THE TIME NAVIGATORS by Gilbert Morris
Travel back in time with Danny and Dixie as they explore unforgettable moments in history.

Young Adult Fiction (12 and up)

CEDAR RIVER DAYDREAMS by Judy Baer
Experience the challenges and excitement of high school life with Lexi Leighton and her friends.

GOLDEN FILLY SERIES by Lauraine Snelling
Tricia Evanston races to become the first female jockey to win the sought-after Triple Crown.

JENNIE MCGRADY MYSTERIES by Patricia Rushford
A contemporary Nancy Drew, Jennie McGrady's sleuthing talents bring back readers again and again.

LIVE! FROM BRENTWOOD HIGH by Judy Baer
The staff of an action-packed teen-run news show explores the love, laughter, and tears of high school life.

THE SPECTRUM CHRONICLES by Thomas Locke
Adventure and romance await readers in this fantasy series set in another place and time.

SPRINGSONG BOOKS by various authors
Compelling love stories and contemporary themes promise to capture the hearts of readers.

WHITE DOVE ROMANCES by Yvonne Lehman
Romance, suspense, and fast-paced action for teens committed to finding pure love.